DON’T DRINK T

By Keith Johnson

This is a work of fiction. All names, characters, businesses, places, incidents and events are a product of the author’s imagination and portrayed in a fictitious manner. Any resemblance to people (living or dead) is purely coincidental.

Dedicated to all the lost ones x.

CONTENTS

Prologue

THIS BOOK FOLLOWS the exploits of six young males and females, some of whom are about to embark on a seven-day Spanish break.

Each character is coming to terms with their problems, and when they eventually cross paths, it will influence their lives forever. Some influences will be for the better and others for the worse.

The one thing that all our characters have in common is that, for one reason or another, they could all do with a holiday. For all of them, it’s a chance to run away from life problems, whether it’s problematic circumstances, problematic people or issues with their own sexuality.

However, holidays don’t always go to plan, and for some, it will be a chance to run into further trouble and endure awkward moments that will have everlasting consequences.

The book is set in 1982. At this time, the gadgets we take for granted today, like mobile phones, personal computers, and satellite navigation, were not readily available.

Windows was still something you just looked through, not something you logged on to, and an apple was something you ate once a day to keep the doctor away. The Internet was in its infant stages; there was no such thing as emails, and small, feathered birds were the only ones who tweeted.

In the UK, the price of a pint of beer was around sixty pence, meaning you could get pretty drunk for a fiver.

The in-vogue recreational drugs amongst the younger population were amphetamines (speed), which came in the form of pills (usually blue) or in powder form, which was known as sulphate. If you wanted to chill out or come down from a high, then Red Lebanese hashish (which had the look and feel of dried-up dog poop) would be your most likely choice. Modern-day highs like cocaine were expensive at the time and mainly confined to the echelons of the wealthy and famous.

The music scene at the time had seen the rise of synthesizer-based bands, and the "New Romantic" bands such as Spandau Ballet and Duran Duran were setting the style and fashion of the era. Survivors from the late seventies punk/new wave era, such as The Clash, The Police and Blondie, were still going strong.

With the advent and popularity of the music video (which was by now a massive industry) and MTV (Music Television), which played music videos in a constant loop, you were always close to seeing and hearing your favourite artists wherever you were. For listening at home, vinyl and cassette tapes were still the main ways people listened to music until compact discs became more freely available and affordable in the mid-eighties.

The term 'Yuppie' was starting to be used widely. This was used to refer to a new group of brash, young, upwardly mobile professionals who were making lots of money from the new, rich pickings that were to be had in and around the money markets of the major cities and also rising property prices. They were living affluent, flashy lifestyles. The excitement that a brighter future may be on the horizon was building throughout the UK.

It's not very often that the prospect of a week's holiday in a foreign land with sand, sea and abundant sunshine shapes the rest of our lives, but that is how it was about to transpire for our unsuspecting young tourists.

Oh, and there's a dog too.

Any similarities to real-life characters or events are purely coincidental.

One

Karate Black Belt

Friday 16th July 1982...

SEBASTIAN HEARD THE screech of tyres outside the house and reluctantly dragged himself up into a sitting position on the bed. Looking out the bedroom window, he saw Terry’s bright red Jaguar outside. It was still rocking slightly as the suspension settled itself after the car’s severe, abrupt halt. A sense of panic coursed through Sebastian as he saw the car door open and Terry’s muscular figure, dressed in grey jogging pants and a black vest, emerge from the driver’s door.

‘Shit!’ Sebastian jumped off the bed with a liveliness that he hadn’t been able to muster together in weeks. He scanned the bedroom for the first time in days, and it hit him what a mess it was in. Empty spirit bottles and beer cans covered the entire surfaces of the bedside cabinet and the dressing table. There were also two ashtrays that were overflowing with cigarette butts and the remains of the countless joints he’d smoked over the last few days. The light green (and recently stained carpet) was strewn with crisp packets, takeaway food cartons, empty cigarette boxes and sweet wrappers.

Don't Drink The Water!

Sebastian had confined himself to the bedroom for six days now, and apart from the occasional outing to buy more junk food, cigarettes, booze and drugs, he'd just lain in bed watching TV. He was feeling very sorry for himself. To him, his young world was falling apart; it felt like his brain was about to explode and that he was under immense pressure. So, in an attempt to forget his woes, he'd been self-medicating with copious amounts of alcohol and Red Leb hashish. At twenty-one years old his life had become a mess of late for reasons, he felt, were out of his control.

The most significant part of the pressure was from Sebastian's father, a solicitor who had decided he would like his son to follow in his footsteps; Sebastian had given in to his father's wishes and was studying law at university. He hated the course and had always thought of himself as more of a number cruncher. He would have much rather have taken on a course in mathematics, chemistry or physics and, if it was down to him alone, his chosen career path would be in teaching or some sort of complicated science. Another problem was that, because of his alcohol and drug abuse and the fact that he'd not been attending his lectures, there were now constant tensions between him and his parents, and they had cut off his allowance until he straightened himself out.

Recently, to get away from his parents, who were by now constantly on his case, he'd been shacking up with his girlfriend Lyndsey. But, because of his self-pitying behaviour, now she'd had enough of him too and had told him that their relationship was over. Lyndsey had also told him that she was going on a week's holiday to Spain without him and that he was to be out of the house by the time she returned; otherwise, there would be consequences.

...

Six days previously...

'WAKE UP YOU lazy bastard!' It was one o'clock in the afternoon, and Lyndsey Fox's voice was raised with frustration as she sat on the side of the bed, slapping repeatedly at Sebastian's face.
With bleary eyes, Sebastian slowly woke up and said, 'What is it? What's wrong?'
'You... That's what's wrong, I want you out!'
Eh? Why? What have I done? I love you.'
'You love me do you? Well, I must say you show it in a very funny way. You haven't loved me for weeks. You can't even get it up. You're always too fucking out of your head.'
'I'll change. It's just because I'm depressed.'
'Depressed?' Lyndsey shook her head in dismay. Having spent most of her childhood not knowing on any given day whether the police would be kicking in the front door to cart her criminal dad, Terry, away or whether he'd have to disappear for weeks on end to lie low and keep his head down had left its mark on her. Along with this constant childhood insecurity, Lyndsey had also endured

watching her mum sink into a state of deep depression for many years. This was mainly due to her husband's frequent, long bouts of absenteeism serving time in prison. During these uncertain periods, Lyndsey's mother (having never been party to where he'd hidden his stolen cash for secrecy reasons) had suffered the indignity of having to rely on hand-outs from friends and family for long periods in order to feed herself and her child until her husband's release.

Terry's last stretch in prison had been a particularly long one. He'd been part of a gang that robbed a security van and had battered the driver viciously, leading to a ten-year sentence. Terry served six years after being paroled on good behaviour and compassionate reasons. Shortly before his release, Lyndsey's mother's depression had worsened into a manic state, and unfortunately, she finally succumbed to her darkness by committing suicide with an overdose of pills.

Part of the condition for Terry's early release had been on the basis that he could take care of his only, and at that time, twelve-year-old daughter. Since his release, Terry had never served another jail term. That didn't mean he'd given up criminality – far from it - he'd just got better at it.

Being an only child, Lyndsey had found the tragedy of her mother's suicide extremely difficult to cope with. The constant emotional battles she'd endured for most of her life meant that Lyndsey could find no sympathy for Sebastian.

'Ahhh, diddums. Poor little rich kid gets depressed because he doesn't want to go back to university. Does depression make you piss the bed?'
There was silence. Sebastian had no answer.
'Well, does it? Like a baby?'
Sebastian craved sympathy and came up with a diversionary tactic. 'I think I've got a brain tumour.'
'A brain tumour?'
'Yeah, I've had a headache for days.'
Lyndsey picked up the half-empty bottle of scotch that was on the bedside cabinet and held it in front of Sebastian's face. 'Or, perhaps it's this? Depression? Brain tumour? You'll never change, you limp-cocked, useless bastard. Look, I'm leaving here in a minute because I'm going to drive to the airport, and then I'm getting on a plane, and then I'm going on holiday to get away from you.
'How long for?'
'A week, and when I get back, you best be gone!'
'Where're you going?'
'None of your business. Just make sure you're gone by the middle of the week, otherwise, I'll be calling my dad.'
'Don't leave me. I'll kill myself!'
'Good! Do yourself and everybody else a favour!'
Lyndsey didn't really mean it and regretted the comment as soon as she'd said it, but it was heat-of-the-moment stuff. Then, with as much empathy she could find at the time, her tone softened as she added, 'Pull yourself together Sebastian, because the way you're going, you are slowly killing

yourself, and you will end up dead.' Lyndsey stood up and walked to the bedroom door. 'Now get your head together and all your stuff, and get out of my house.'

'Please don't leave me. You'll feel really guilty when you find out I'm dead. You know you will.'

Lyndsey paused in the doorway and shook her head with disdain. 'Just fuck off Sebastian.' She left the bedroom and went downstairs.

Sebastian sat up in bed and took a swig of scotch straight from the bottle, and finding a half-smoked joint in the ashtray beside him, he lit it up. He ruffled his unkempt, greasy, chocolate-coloured, long hair that reached down his back between his shoulder blades. Then, feeling even more sorry for himself than he did before, he started to sob.

A couple of minutes later, he heard the front door slam and watched through the window as Lyndsey left the house without saying goodbye. He looked on as she loaded her suitcase into the trunk of her Vauxhall Astra car. Lyndsey opened the driver's door and, with a bit of wriggle, she settled into the seat and switched on the ignition. Sebastian opened the bedroom window fully and shouted, 'DON'T LEAVE ME! I LOVE YOU!' Sebastian continued to sob uncontrollably as he watched the car pulling away.

...

Friday 16th continued...

TO MAKE SURE that her wishes with regards to Sebastian’s departure had been acted upon Lyndsey had decided early one evening, on the penultimate day of her holiday, to make a speculative call to her home from a payphone in Benidorm. She didn’t know why she’d felt the compulsion to do so, but she wanted reassurance that she would be returning to an empty house. To her shock and unpleasant surprise, Sebastian had picked up.
‘You bastard... I told you to get out!’
‘But I...’
‘I’m calling my dad.’
Lyndsey didn’t allow him to speak further, and she slammed the phone down in anger without saying another word. She immediately called her dad, Terry. They chatted for a while about how her holiday was going, the weather, the food and all the other usual pleasantries that people talk about when they’re on holiday. After the small talk had finished, Lyndsey told Terry the real reason for her call - and about her problem with Sebastian
‘Consider it done,’ had been the last words Terry had spoken before the line went dead. Lyndsey’s money had run out, and her time on the payphone was up. She had meant to tell her dad not to hurt Sebastian as (having been together for over a year and despite whatever it was that Sebastian had turned into) she did still have some feelings towards him. Lyndsey pulled her purse from her petite, glittering silver handbag, and after some

frantic searching she found another hundred peseta coin. She tried to ring her dad again, but there was no answer at the other end. Little did she know that Terry was already on the case, and it was now too late to do anything about it. She didn't hate Sebastian she was just frustrated by his laziness and latest lifestyle choices.
When they'd first met, Sebastian was in a good place. He came from a good family, and Lyndsey hoped that she might find some stability after her troubled and difficult upbringing. She pushed the payphone's coin return button, but nothing came out.

...

TERRY HAD JUST returned from his afternoon run and was still hot and sweaty. Immediately after putting the phone down to Lyndsey, he grabbed his keys, quick-stepped out the front door into his Jaguar XJ12, switched on the ignition and booted the accelerator, setting off at speed to resolve the situation in hand.
The suburban streets of Manchester were unusually quiet, and Terry estimated it would only be a five-minute drive to the little, two-bedroom house that he'd bought for his daughter using money from his ill-gotten gains. The last few years had been very lucrative for Terry – he'd pulled off some big jobs and, so far, he'd managed to keep his stash (and himself) out of reach of the long arm of the law.

The house that Terry had bought for Lyndsey was, for him, a kind of recompense for him having been in and out of prison during most of her childhood years.

As he drove Terry didn't feel anger, he just felt annoyed that some posh-kid loser was taking advantage of his daughter's generosity and kindly nature. He'd already decided in the back of his head that if showing his annoyance and irritation wasn't enough to settle the issue, then a show of anger and violence would have to ultimately follow. Terry turned on the radio and "This Town Ain't Big Enough For The Both Of Us" by Sparks was playing. Terry sang along and giggled to himself at his disastrous attempts to reach the same high notes as the track's singer.

...

RIGHT NOW, SEBASTIAN'S situation wasn't looking good, and in his panic, Sebastian tried to gather large amounts of the debris around the bedroom in armfuls and hide the evidence in the wardrobe. But, as he tried to open the wardrobe door (using the little finger of his right hand because it was the only free digit he had available to him), he dropped the lot on the floor again. 'Fuck it!' Sebastian said under his breath. Then, he rolled over the width of the bed commando style while cautiously trying to stay out of view of the large window. Sebastian hoped that if Terry looked up from the street he wouldn't be able to spot him. He knelt on the floor and nervously peered over the window sill. He saw Terry striding purposefully down the garden path, and the idea occurred to Sebastian that the best way forward would be to just not answer the door. When his unwanted visitor rang the doorbell, there would be no answer, and after a while, Terry would just go away. Sebastian crouched down and then rolled himself into a ball on the floor, wrapping his hands tightly around his head. Sebastian waited for the sound of the doorbell - which, of course, he would ignore.

What Sebastian hadn't realised was that Terry had his own set of keys to the house. Sebastian, staying completely still and silent, heard the sound of Terry's key turning in the lock. He came over in a cold sweat of fear and felt a sudden urge to urinate. Sebastian heard the door open. Then, a squelching sound from the soles of Terry's trainers on the laminate flooring as he walked around downstairs, opening and closing doors as he looked for signs of life.

Then, there was the familiar sound of the creaking staircase as Terry ascended up the stairs onto the small landing. Sebastian jumped to his feet. He headed towards the bedroom door, and on the way, he grabbed a chair from under the dressing table. Sebastian had intended to jam it under the door handle, thereby forcing the door shut so that it couldn't be opened from the outside. But, before he could get the chair into position, the handle turned, the door opened, and he was confronted by Terry.

Sebastian's bladder gave way, and a large patch of urine started to become apparent on the front of his light blue jeans.
'What are you doing with that?' Terry said with a puzzled look at the sight of Sebastian standing before him still holding the chair in mid-air.
'I was just moving it over here.'
'Why?'
Sebastian noticed that the puzzled look on Terry's face had turned more into an expression of mild annoyance. Sebastian scanned Terry's physique, taking notice of his muscular chest and shoulders that were accentuated by the tight, black vest that arced over the well-formed shoulder muscles just below his thick neck.
Terry was a fit-looking forty-eight-year-old. He wasn't a tall man (he was only five feet nine inches), but he'd spent countless hours in prison gyms in an effort to relieve the boredom and get through his time inside without incident. This meant his physique more than made up for his lack of height. Also, the fact that he had continued with his regular exercise and workout regime when on the outside meant Terry's shoulders were exceptionally broad. So much so, that they seemed in some way out of proportion with the rest of his stature. His wide chest was powerful with well-formed pectoral muscles. Doing regular five-mile runs kept Terry's waist trim, and his thick thighs noticeably stretched the cloth of his jogging bottoms. His blond, crew-cut hairstyle that was

slightly greying at the close-shaven sides only added to his intimidating appearance.

In contrast, Sebastian was tall and gangly, and there wasn't much sign of a toned muscle anywhere on his body. He had never had any interest in gyms, exercise or sports of any kind. There was a time when he was fourteen years old (after having been bullied at school and in an effort to give him confidence) when he'd enrolled on a karate class. However, his gangly limbs (which he'd never seemed to be able to coordinate very well) and his lack of muscle power meant it was a short-lived experience, and he only passed the first grading before becoming utterly bored of the whole thing.

'I didn't like it where it was,' Sebastian replied without any conviction.

'Put it back.'

Sebastian duly complied and gingerly returned the chair to its rightful place under the dresser.

'Have you pissed yourself?' Terry pointed at the newly formed wet patch on Sebastian's jeans.

Red-faced with embarrassment, Sebastian struggled with a suitable reply for a second. 'No, I spilled my drink.'

'Looks like piss to me. Anyway, let's get onto the matter in hand. Lyndsey wants you out.

'I live here.'

'Not anymore you don't.'

'I'm not leaving. I've got nowhere else to go.'

'Yes, you are leaving. Now, I want to be nice, so why don't you get your stuff and I'll drive you round to your mum and dad's?'
'I don't want to go to my mum and dad's... I want to stay here.' Sebastian's voice started to crack with emotion. 'I love Lyndsey.'
'Well, she doesn't love you. So, let me make myself clear. There is no room for negotiation, and you *are* leaving, whether it's the easy way or whether it's the hard way.'
'I'm not going. I'll explain everything and work it out with Lyndsey when she gets back,' Sebastian said with fearful defiance.
'Right then, we'll see about that.'
Terry took a step forward. Sebastian flinched, took a nervous backward step, and, with the bit of self-pride that he had left, decided to play his trump card.
'Don't come near me. I have to warn you I'm a karate black belt,' Sebastian lied. Then he followed up his words by taking up a sideways, karate-style stance (that was correct to the best of his memory) and started to rock backwards and forwards on the balls of his feet in an attempt to make him look like he was the karate expert he claimed.
'Really?' Terry stroked his stubbly chin with his left hand thoughtfully. 'Karate black belt eh?'
'Yeah.'
'Oh dear...' Terry continued to stroke his chin as if seriously mulling the situation over.
Sebastian thought Terry's aggression was subsiding and that his face had taken on a softer

expression. It was kind of hard to tell because Terry's dark-brown eyes (so dark they almost looked like black holes) that never showed much sign of any emotion were not now aimed directly at Sebastian and were, instead, focused downward, looking at the floor. Terry's dead eyes gave very little away. But, Sebastian convinced himself that a look of genuine trepidation and concern had come over his antagonist. Sebastian started to believe that his ploy was working. What he failed to realise was that Terry didn't know anxiety or fear - they weren't part of his emotional repertoire.

Without any outward sign of a change in mood, Terry switched to angry mode in a millisecond, and his left hand, the one he'd been using to stroke his chin, became a fist. The jab he launched forward was lightning-fast and smashed into Sebastian's nose. The strike was delivered with uncanny accuracy and power by the smaller man. Then, before Sebastian could react, a thumping right hook landed squarely on his jaw, and he was sent crashing to the floor.

Terry stood over Sebastian, glaring down at him.

'KARATE THAT YOU DOPE-HEAD CUNT!'

Terry snarled with menace, and then he stamped on Sebastian's face just for good measure, splattering blood from his already broken nose even further across his face.

...

EVEN IN HIS semi-conscious state, Sebastian could feel the thud every time his head dropped limply onto all of the twelve stairs as Terry dragged him by his feet down the staircase. Continuing to drag his victim through the still-open front door, Terry dropped Sebastian's legs unceremoniously at the start of the garden path as he went back to close it.

While Terry was momentarily distracted, Sebastian lifted his head and then tried to push himself up to his feet. The idea was to run to a neighbour's house and get them to call the police. However, being still in a daze, Sebastian's coordination let him down, and he fell backwards, bashing his head once more on the hard, stone garden path. Terry returned, grabbed Sebastian by the feet once more and proceeded to drag him the rest of the way up the path towards his Jaguar car.

'Oh, my God!' Shrieked a middle-aged lady in a horrified tone. The small poodle dog that was walking at her side started to let out a continuous volley of high-pitched barks. 'What's happened to that poor man?' The state of Sebastian's smashed face was a shocking, violent spectacle.

'He fell over,' Terry said. Then, with his trainer-clad right foot, he prodded Sebastian in the testicles (they were an easy target between his splayed legs) with enough force to show he meant business. 'Go on, tell her.'

Sebastian hesitated for a second. Then, deciding his position was pretty much hopeless, he complied weakly. 'I fell over.'

Terry gave the lady a knowing smile and a wink of the eye. Feeling awkward and unsure about how to deal with the situation that she had unwittingly stumbled into, the lady decided it would be wise not to stick around much longer. So, without another word, she hurriedly carried on her way.
Terry opened the rear door of his Jaguar and dragged Sebastian up and onto the back seat of the Jaguar. 'And don't fucking bleed on my leather seats!' He slammed the door shut and opened the driver's door. But, before he got in, Terry grabbed a beige cloth that he used to wipe the windscreen from the door pocket. 'Here, have this.' Terry reached into back over the driver's seat and shoved the cloth roughly into Sebastian's bloodied face.
Terry jumped into position behind the steering wheel, started the engine and pumped the accelerator a couple of times, listening admiringly to the roar of the Jaguar's powerful, twelve-cylinder engine. He shifted the auto-gearbox lever into drive and sped off. As he drove away, his thoughts turned to how the day's events had worked out well. Another job had been jobbed. Lyndsey had her house back, and in the process, Terry had actually enjoyed himself immensely.
"Start Me Up" by the Rolling Stones came on the radio. Mick Jagger started his lyrics... "*If you start me up... If you start me up, I'll never stop*". Terry sang along merrily - like a man without a care in the world.
After a ten-minute drive, Terry stopped the Jaguar outside Sebastian's parent's house. He pulled

Sebastian out of the rear of the car and threw him forcefully through the wooden garden gate, breaking the rickety, metal latch in the process. Sebastian felt a dull pain in his buttocks as he landed heavily on his backside.
'Now, be a good boy... Fuck off... And don't bother my daughter again. And remember, if your mum and dad ask, you fell over, right? I don't want any grief from this, because if I do get any grief it won't be just your nose that gets broken.'
Looking at Sebastian's pitiful state and the fear still lurking behind his rapidly swelling and blackening eyes, Terry felt reasonably reassured that his warning would be heeded. So, pleased with a job well done, he jumped back into the car, and without a second look back, he started to drive away.
Mustering all the energy he had left within him, Sebastian pulled himself up onto his feet and shouted, 'I'LL GET THE POLICE ON YOU, YOU FUCKING BASTARD!'
The Jaguar skidded to a halt and then reversed back up the road rapidly. Terry wound down the electric passenger side window and gave Sebastian one more menacing glare. 'What did you just say?'
There was a pause as Sebastian weighed up his options and came to the swift conclusion that they were very limited. 'Nothing.'
'Thought so.' The car window started to close slowly, and when it was completely shut, Terry sped off into the distance.

...

BACK IN BENIDORM, Lyndsey strolled along the Avenida Madrid and, looking out at the calm of the Mediterranean Sea, she wondered if Sebastian had any inkling of the imminent storm he'd let himself in for. Lyndsey knew the kind of violence that her dad was capable of. Knowing that there was nothing she could possibly do about it now, she sighed. *What will be, will be*. Her thoughts suddenly turned to the greedy phone box that had eaten all of her hundred pesetas. The machine had not given any refund into the returned coins slot even though her dad hadn't picked up. *Fucking Spanish*, she thought, *that's enough for a vodka and tonic.*

She meandered a little further and then slipped off her silver sandals. Stepping down onto the warm, golden sand of Levante Beach, she sat down on the edge of the promenade, lit a cigarette and admired the view. The sun was halfway down, and it was still light under a cloudless, blue sky. The sea was calm, with just insignificant, white-tipped waves rolling in. Lyndsey could see a few early-evening swimmers further out. There were still children in the shallows having fun and splashing about in the water. The sun was still strong – intense enough that she could feel tiny beads of sweat forming on the exposed skin of her face, arms and legs.

After finishing her cigarette and a few minutes with her thoughts, Lyndsey stood up and stepped back up onto terra firma. She brushed the sand off her feet, slipped her sandals back on and after walking a bit further down, she took a left turn into a side street. Stopping in front of a clothes shop window, she lifted her sunglasses onto the top of her forehead and studied her reflection. The peroxide-blonde, bobbed hairstyle that she had curled tightly at the bottom so that it tucked under her cheekbones and along the base of her neck was looking good. She pulled up the sequinned, black boob tube that accentuated her full, 34D, braless bosom so that it was equally adjusted on both sides under her armpits. Pouting her heart-shaped lips that tilted up at the edges and gave the impression of a forever smile, Lyndsey couldn’t help thinking that the pink lipstick matched the colour of her short skirt almost perfectly. At only five feet, three inches tall, her squat frame, along with her slightly chunky but firm and, by now, lightly sun-kissed legs, meant that she wasn’t really model material. Lyndsey had given up all ambitions of being a model or a beauty queen a long time ago to pursue a career in hairdressing. However, now in the last of her teenage years, she couldn’t help but think she was looking pretty good. The sparkling silver sandals that matched her handbag just completed a successful look.

Lyndsey took a time-out for a short period of window shopping, and then she rejoined the main drag along the seafront. She only had to walk a short distance before reaching The Beach Rock Bar.

As Lyndsey entered The Beach Rock, she caught a glimpse of Jude and Danny out of the corner of her eye. The two boys were sitting at a high table at the other end of the busy, noisy venue. She headed for the area of the bar where her new-found girlfriends were seated at a large round table.

On the way over, Lyndsey had to manoeuvre her way around a bikini-clad, mid-fortyish-looking woman with a big bottom and sunburnt back. The woman had obviously consumed vast amounts of alcohol during the afternoon and had now collapsed in a drunken heap on the dance floor. The woman was scratching at the wooden floor in an effort to drag herself back to her table. She was desperately trying to get some purchase by attempting to dig in with her bright red, painted fingernails. But, her large, fatty breasts, which had by this time dislodged themselves from her skimpy bikini top, were preventing any forward movement because her skin was sticking to the tacky, drink-stained floor.

An overweight man with vast amounts of greying body hair and dressed in oversized shorts and a vest (who Lyndsey could only assume was the collapsed woman's husband) was sitting at a corner table on the terrace with another couple. He shouted in a strong Yorkshire accent, 'GET UP YOU SILLY COW!' Taking a large swig from his pint of beer and making no attempt to get up or assist his stricken wife, he continued. 'YOU

BLOODY EMEBRASSMENT. I TOLD YOU NOT TO HAVE THAT LAST SODDING GIN AND TONIC DIDN’T I?’

Having negotiated her way to the bar, Lyndsey ordered herself a large vodka and tonic. She took a couple of quick sips and joined the melee that was her large group of girlfriends. She just hoped that the evening would go how she’d planned it in her head. If it did, then a few hours later, she, Jude and Danny were in for a wild, exciting time.

Two

Word Games

Friday 9th July 1982...

THE TIME WAS just approaching four o'clock in the afternoon. Kieran Maw stood in front of the round, decorative mirror on his office wall and adjusted his tie. Producing a comb from his inside jacket pocket, he ran it through his shoulder-length, Brylcreemed, black but slightly greying, swept-back hair. He was proud of his flowing locks and didn't mind going grey (even if it was somewhat premature) because, at forty-six years old, it was only to be expected to a certain degree. To his mind, the multiple streaks of almost pure white only played to complement his handsome good looks. All this, put together with his trim torso, which was kept in shape by regularly playing tennis at his local club, gave him what he considered to be a rather distinguished managerial look. At least, that's how he saw himself; in truth, he was a relatively unattractive man with slightly rounded shoulders and a noticeable pot belly.

Kieran had left his previous job delivering stationery supplies to offices and banks to join Superior Sanitary Supplies as a salesman almost ten years ago. After five years he was head of his

own sales team. Then, three years after that, he was promoted to his current level of senior sales executive. Kieran enjoyed his job mainly because he just loved to sell. It was the process of chatting up prospective clients. He would promise them the world if need be, thus enticing them away from a competitor's grasp, and then reel them in and take their money.
For Kieran, selling was not only a challenge, but also a thrill. He considered himself excellent at his job, charming and highly intelligent. He also believed it had been lucky, for both himself and Superior Sanitary Supplies, that he'd found his true vocation in life. In his mind it was these attributes that had led to his rapid rise up the ranks within the company. To others (including many of his work colleagues and staff), his demeanour and self-belief were interpreted as arrogance, come conceit, and his quick promotions mainly down to being a boardroom arse-licker.
Turning away from the mirror, Kieran took off his suit jacket and draped it over the back of his office chair. He brushed away a few specks of embarrassing dandruff from the dark-brown jacket's collar and then sat down at his desk. He spent a few moments adjusting his desktop nameplate that read, "Kieran A. Maw", with "Senior Sales Executive" in smaller letters underneath so that it was sitting nice and straight directly in front of him. Superior Sanitary Supplies wasn't a large conglomerate or anything like that, and it wasn't like the staff that Kieran considered

his minions didn’t know who he was, so it could be construed that the desktop nameplate was unnecessary. However, to Kieran, it added some kudos and importance to his senior role within the company and his ultimate superiority over the sales team.
Kieran glanced briefly at the framed photo of his wife and two daughters. It was the same photo that he confined to the desk drawer when he and his plumpish, thirty-nine-year-old PA Sally had their sexual liaisons. These marital misdemeanours were usually acted out either on or over Kieran’s desk. By hiding the photo away it made it feel like he wasn’t cheating on, or hurting, those who loved him. Kieran adjusted his positioning in his swivelling leather office chair and adjusted the height slightly with the lever on the side until he felt comfortable. When he felt happy that everything was in order, Kieran pressed the talk button on his intercom.
‘You can send Jude in now Sally,’ he announced to his PA who was busily typing at her desk just the other side of the door.
A few seconds later, Jude Cooper entered the room wearing a dark blue suit with a red tie. Jude was a tall, handsome, mixed-race lad who liked to keep his tightly-knit, curly, black hair cropped close to his skull. He kept his bordering-on fourteen-stone, thickset frame in shape with regular visits to the gym and playing football for his local Saturday league side.

Jude's upbringing had been a difficult one. His white mother and black father had struggled to cope with the pressure of bringing up a mixed-race child amidst the stereotyping and racial prejudices that were rife in the nineteen-sixties and early seventies. His parents' pressured relationship started to fall apart when Jude was six years old. One day, his father had got on a flight to Jamaica, where the mainstay of his family still lived, and never returned.

Jude's mother was left feeling lost and alone. With very little money coming in, she and Jude sank close to a state of destitution. She turned to alcohol to ease the pain. Then, when his mother could no longer cope with the stresses and strains of her own life, let alone the added pressures of bringing up a young child, Jude took a wayward turn. His life became a mess. His mother was almost incapable of providing for any of their everyday needs (due to her alcoholism) and Jude took to shoplifting to feed and water them both. Eventually, too many brushes with the law sealed Jude's fate. The authorities that-be were informed, and at the age of eleven, for Jude's general well-being and to stop Jude from slipping into more severe criminality, a decision was made to take him into care. Jude's mother didn't put up much of a fight to keep her son – the alcohol addiction was too strong.

Life in a North London children's home wasn't easy, and it took time to adjust. Jude had to find toughness within him – more than he'd ever shown previously. Jude's mixed-race status was used against him many times, and he was frequently harangued with racial abuse (from both white kids and black kids) within the children's home and at school. Subsequently, he'd had to fight his corner, verbally and with his fists, more times than any vulnerable young boy should have to.

At the age of twelve Jude had been put in the care of middle-aged, white foster parents. But the married couple ran a strict, ultra-religious home and the constant bible-bashing was stifling. One day, after an argument and Jude mouthing a string of profanities, his surrogate father had tried to take a cane to him. As the man approached wielding his cane, Jude, who was a big lad for a twelve-year-old, split the man's lip with a well-aimed punch and ran away from the house.

These experiences had hardened Jude's character and, as he entered his teenage years, he became determined to turn his life around. Jude was extremely proud of the fact that, despite the bad cards life had dealt him, he'd managed to put his head down at school and achieve a good level of academic and sporting success.

Recently, Jude had made attempts to see if he could regain some form of relationship with his mother. However, she now had a new partner who was a fellow alcoholic. Neither Jude's mother nor her new partner had any work, and they relied on state handouts to keep them in booze and cigarettes. Therefore, every meeting just dragged Jude down. They were always a pretty miserable, arduous experience and he had no plans of visiting his mother again anytime in the foreseeable future. Jude's largely circumstantial fall and subsequent self-induced rise meant he didn't suffer fools gladly. A stark glare with his piercing, almost fluorescent, blue eyes (which were handsomely set off by his coffee-coloured, unblemished skin) was usually enough to let his adversaries know he meant business. However, although when riled he took no prisoners, he had an ability to turn on the charm when need be and also a sharp, if sometimes slightly cruel, wit.

'Ah, Jude dear boy...' Kieran ushered with his left arm towards the vacant vinyl chair on the other side of the desk, 'Sit ye down.'

Before taking his seat, Jude stretched out his arm and offered his right hand for a shake. Kieran got to his feet and, leaning over his desk, accepted the offered hand. After the brief handshake, they both took their seats. Kieran leaned right back in his chair and folded his arms. Jude noticed a smug, self-assured smile spreading across Kieran's face. Kieran decided to start the conversation with a bit of friendly chit-chat. 'So, a little bird tells me you're off on your holidays tomorrow?'

'Yep.'

'Well, I'll bet you're looking forward to that; where are you off to?'

'Spain, and yeah, I can't wait.'

'Whereabouts in Spain?'

'Benidorm.'

'Oh, I see. There are more... How can I put this... There are more cultural parts of Spain you know?' Kieran was being deliberately condescending. 'But that said, I have to say, why am I not surprised?' Jude responded to Kieran's deliberate slight on the offensive. 'Oh yeah, and what exactly do you mean by that?'
'Just that... Well... You know...'
'No, I don't.'
Kieran realised he'd dug a bit of a hole for himself and decided to change the subject. 'Well, let's forget about that for now. So, now we're all done with the niceties, it's time to get down to the business at hand. So, Jude, are you aware of the reason I've called you into the office today?' Kieran picked up a packet of cigarettes lying on top of his desk, pulled one out and lit it up.
Jude shrugged his shoulders. 'Sort of. The word is that you're not happy with some of my business decisions.'
Kieran unfolded his arms, and the smug smile started to subside. He threw his elbows down onto his desk, leaned his head and shoulders forward towards Jude and stared into his eyes intently. There was a slight pause before Kieran took on a more aggressive demeanour and tone. 'The word is right!' Kieran blew the smoke from his cigarette straight into Jude's face. Jude knew that Kieran was deliberately trying to intimidate him. Jude also knew what was coming next. Since he'd joined the company three years ago, straight from leaving school, he'd sat through plenty of similar meetings

with Kieran in the past. Jude had never liked Kieran but had to tolerate him because he was his boss. The fact was they'd seen eye to eye on very little recently.
Things had started to come to a head over the last year when Jude had been let out in the sales field on his own and allowed to negotiate contracts with clients in his own right. To Jude, his boss was purely interested in maximising profits in the short term with little regard for keeping customers happy and satisfied. If a client decided to drop out of a contract, then go out there and find another, better deal with someone else - that was Kieran's mantra. Jude's ideology was different. He liked to think he saw the bigger picture in ensuring his customers were content and would stay loyal to the company. He looked at customer relations in the long term. And, if that sometimes means having to take a minor hit in profits every now and again to keep them happy, then so be it. Jude had always thought of Kieran as being a bit of a slime-ball and, as well as being patronising, Kieran also had a tendency to try and belittle the members of the sales team ranked below him. This was the third time in the last two months that Jude had been summoned into the office for a lecture on his sales technique.
Jude was by now tired of his capabilities being called into question and the thought that maybe it was time for a change of job and a new start had entered his head many times recently. The prospect of leaving and having to find another job didn't scare him in the slightest. On leaving school, he'd

had three interviews with would-be employers and, with the school grades he'd achieved and by using his natural charm, he had been offered the job by each one. Eventually, he'd plumped for Superior Sanitary Supplies because it was the best paid. When he reached sixteen, Jude was too old to stay in the care home and had been turfed out to find his own way in the world. This meant finding himself a place to live. Jude found a room in a house which he shared with three other tenants. Taking into account that he now had rent and bills to pay, and also the experience of his hand-to-mouth early childhood, he wanted to end up (after all his outgoings) with little money to spend on having a good time. But, if push came to shove and his time at Superior Sanitary Supplies was up, Jude was confident in his own abilities and was reasonably sure he wouldn't have much trouble finding another job.

Kieran continued. 'So, what's going on with this Prestige Hotels contract thing? I hear you've taken back a heap load of toilet tissue for credit.'

'Yes, I have.'

'For why?'

'They said they weren't happy with the quality of the product… Said they'd had complaints from the guests and their own staff. So, to keep them happy, I replaced the stock with the luxury, soft range.'

There was a short silence as Kieran extinguished his cigarette in the ashtray. 'At a loss?' Kieran looked at Jude's through squinting, unbelieving

eyes. Then, Kieran shook his head mockingly at what he believed to be Jude’s incompetency.
Jude let out a deep sigh. ‘Yes, we lose a bit on the bog rolls...’
‘Bog rolls?’ Kieran took on a startled expression and sat bolt upright in his chair, ‘I hope you don’t talk to the clients like that. No wonder we’re losing money.’
‘Shut up.’
‘Don’t tell me to...’
‘Just shut up. As I was saying, yes we lose a bit on the *bog rolls*, but we’re still supplying them with the shower gels, the shampoos, the bars of soap, the sanitisers and all the rest of it, so overall, the contract still makes a healthy profit.’ While waiting for Kieran’s retort, Jude leaned over the desk, peeled off one of Kieran’s post-it notes from the pile in front of him and, pulling a pen from his inside jacket pocket, startled doodling.
‘I employ you as a salesman, not a taker-backer, refund man! What was the problem with the said *toilet tissue*?’
‘You want me to be graphic?’
‘Be as graphic as you like.’
‘They said it wasn’t strong enough, which, reading between the lines, I guess means people’s fingers were going through it. People were getting shitty fingers.’
‘That’s ridiculous!’
‘Really? Okay, so what would you have done? How would you have dealt with it? What would you have said to them?’ Jude only looked up for a

brief moment and then continued with his doodles. He was rapidly losing interest in this conversation. 'What would I have done?' Kieran paused for thought, 'I'd have said something like… Oh, I don't know…' He wanted to make a quick response in order to show Jude what a great salesman's brain he had, but he was struggling. Kieran suddenly found inspiration. 'I would have said…' He unfolded his arms, turned his head to the side and then spoke as if the client was sitting next to him, 'Are you sure the product is being used in the correct manner?' Almost as soon as he'd uttered the words, Kieran knew he'd said something rather silly and unrealistic. But, before he could retract his words, Jude looked Kieran straight in the eye and, with the irritation that was building inside him, Jude launched his barrage.

'We're talking about bog rolls Kieran for fuck's sake! Oh, right, so now I'm supposed to say something to the hotel manager like, *are you sure your customers know how to wipe their own arses*?'

'You know that's not what…'

Jude stopped Kieran in his tracks to let off another volley. 'Perhaps I should've set up a kiosk in the hotel foyer giving demonstrations on arse wiping techniques!' Jude stood up, bent over and pretended to wipe his own bottom. 'There, you see Mr Jones?' Acting like the imaginary Mr Jones was in front of him in the office, Jude continued. 'That's how to wipe your arse. You've been getting it wrong all these years… Tut-tut.'

Kieran was reeling. He'd never experienced a sales meeting like this before. He raised his voice.
'That's enough Jude! You caught me on the hop a bit there, but I know I would've…'
'You're talking shit - if you'll pardon the pun'.
'Don't you dare...'
Jude, waving Kieran's angry comment aside, interrupted once more. 'To be honest Kieran I really don't give a fuck anymore. How about we play a little word game?'
'What are you talking about?'
'Do you like word games Kieran?'
Kieran looked confused by the sudden change of subject. He'd lost control of the meeting and didn't have a clue where this was going. 'What's that got to do with anything?'
'I'm just asking. Do you like word games?'
'Well, I can't say I'm particularly fussed. Why?'
'That's a shame because I've just been looking at your nameplate, and if you play about with the letters a bit, it's surprising what you can make out of "KIERAN A. MAW". By the way, it's an interesting name, "Maw". Do you know where it originates from?'
'I believe it's an ancient Scottish name, but I fail to see what this has to do with anything. Can we just...'
Jude stood up abruptly, and with an outstretched right arm, he pushed the post-it note he'd been doodling on under Kieran's nose. 'You see? Play about with the letters a bit and "KIERAN A. MAW" becomes…'

'I can't see it, it's too small.'
Jude moved the note closer to Kieran's eyes.
Kieran was still struggling to read it and took his time mouthing the words slowly. 'I… AM… A… WANKER.'
'You said it. Clever... Eh? And it suits, doesn't it?'
Jude pointed down at Kieran's nameplate. 'Maybe it's about time you got that changed.'
For once, Kieran was at a loss for words. Jude continued with one last volley. 'Look, fuck you Kieran and fuck your job!' And with that, he turned around and quick-stepped toward the office door.
'YOU'LL NEVER MAKE A SALESMAN! YOU'LL NEVER AMOUNT TO ANYTHING!'
Kieran was beside himself with rage at having been humiliated.
'Better than being a complete wanker though,' Jude said without turning round. He gave Kieran the middle finger from behind his back and slammed the door behind him.
A few seconds passed before Kieran shouted, 'YOU USELESS HALF-CHAT BASTARD!' It was his attempt at regaining some of his severely hurt pride from the situation.
The office door reopened so abruptly that it almost fell off its hinges, and Jude strode in. His fists were clenched tight as he rapidly approached the desk.
Kieran instinctively put his hands defensively in front of his face. He saw Jude's right fist cocked back and ready to throw the first blow. Jude's brain was racing frantically, and in a split second, he

decided that a night in a police cell wasn't the way forward and, besides, he'd heard worse before.
'You ain't fucking worth it,' Jude said with a disdainful shake of the head. Jude's piercing, ferocious glare meant Kieran was struck dumb momentarily which, combined with his fear, prevented him from even considering a retort. Jude turned away and left the office.
As Jude walked out into the fresh air, leaving the Superior Sanitary Supplies offices for the last time, he came over with an inner glow of self-satisfaction that he hadn't felt for a long time. What he'd just done wasn't going to get him much of a job reference in the future, but, *boy-oh-boy*, for the time being did it feel good. He jumped on a bus and headed home to his room.
Once home, he showered and prepared himself a quick bite to eat. Then, once availed of pale blue denim jeans, a white Fred Perry polo shirt and grey, suede Gola trainers, he headed for the pub.

Three

A Nice Cup of Tea

Saturday 10th July 1982...

DANNY ACKERMAN WOKE up abruptly on this particular Saturday morning.
The abruptness of his awakening was partly due to the fact that he was excited about going on holiday with his two mates, Jude and Brian, but mainly due to the half a gram of speed that he'd consumed the previous evening.
Danny hadn't slept very well at all, constantly waking up and then dozing back off again for a short while. He glanced at the clock on his bedside cabinet and saw that it was still early and the time was just approaching eight o'clock. He'd just about be getting up by now on a work day in order for a nine o'clock start at the estate agents office. His office was only a ten-minute walk away from his house. So, getting up an hour before work gave him plenty of time to get his ablutions out of the way and for a shower every morning. But today, all Danny needed to worry about was getting packed and ready for his upcoming holiday in Spain. The flight out to Alicante wasn't until mid-afternoon, so there was still plenty of time and, with that

thought, he attempted to get back off to sleep again.
Another ten minutes passed, and Danny realised that it was no use trying for more sleep. The amount of sulphate he'd dabbed the night before and the excitement of the holiday was just too much. So, he just lay on his bed for a while with eyes wide open. The thoughts of good times ahead were coming thick and fast. Then, for reasons Danny couldn't explain, he felt a stirring in his loins which he couldn't stop, and his cock began to rise of its own accord.
This erection was going to need getting rid of.
Danny took his manhood in hand and started to masturbate; slowly at first and then with ever-quickening strokes. The strange thing about all the previous night's sulphate was that it had kind of numbed his cock. The lack of feeling and the extra staying power that comes with it meant that Danny knew that ejaculation was a long way off. He decided that some extra stimulation would be required.
Danny swung his legs out of bed and went over to his wardrobe where he had a few pornographic magazines hidden in an old shoe box. Before opening the wardrobe he gave himself a once over in the large mirror that was attached to the door. He couldn't help thinking that his fully erect, circumcised cock was an impressive sight - even if he did say so himself. He noticed that his eyes were looking bleary, a bit bloodshot and heavy from the lack of sleep. His ordinarily neat, short and sharply

parted jet-black hair was looking ruffled from all the night's tossing and turning. Danny played with it for a few seconds, trying to pat it down and give it a general tidy-up. Then, he ran his fingers across the top of his head to try to restore a partial parting. As he did so, he saw that his thick, black eyebrows were getting close to meeting in the middle of his forehead again; they were going to need some attention with his clippers later on in the day. Danny ran his index over his fulsome lips, which he was very proud of. Indeed, he considered them his best facial feature. Therefore, he always took care of them by carrying a tube of lip moisturiser with him wherever he went and applied the cream regularly throughout the day. Danny thought that his lips felt a bit dry and considered moisturising them there and then. But, a quick look down at his taught groin meant that, for the time being, his cock was the thing that needed his immediate attention.

Danny shuffled through his porn magazines, pausing for a while when he came across his one and only gay man's publication. He'd purchased it on a whim and kept meaning to get rid of it. But, deciding that the gay magazine might be worth another look, he tossed it behind him onto the bed. Danny was in two minds as to whether the gay mag would be enough to finish the job, so he decided that some female porn was needed too. Once he'd found some material that he considered suitable, he got back into bed.

Danny flicked through the pages of both porno magazines at speed and started to masturbate furiously once more. Still there was no inkling of an impending climax. Danny closed his eyes tightly, pulled the bed sheets over him and thought of some of the girls he'd had sexual encounters with.
To Danny's mild irritation, the thoughts of girls began to intermingle with thoughts of boys and some of the homosexual experiences from his teenage years. They had started on a scout camping trip Danny had been on when he was thirteen. In the darker hours one evening, Danny and his male tent-mate had engaged in some in-depth conversations about masturbation and oral sex. For two relatively newly pubescent boys, the talk had led to them both being in a state of high excitement and ended with them finding various ways of gratifying each other. After their return home they had continued with their gratification sessions for another six months. Then, one day the secret relationship came to an abrupt end when the other boy told Danny he'd decided what they were up to wasn't proper or decent. So, in an effort to find what he considered normality and to conform, the other boy went about finding himself a girlfriend. The two boys never spoke to each other again.
Danny quickly cast the thoughts from his head because he did feel a certain amount of shame about the illicit encounters. He reassured himself that most boys had probably had sexual feelings for other boys at some time during their teenage years.

A teenage boy's pubescent years are complicated and confusing. So, getting another boy to wank you off or give you a blow job during those crazy, hormonal years doesn't make you a poof – *does it?* However, whenever Danny's thoughts turned to those days they were always followed by pangs of guilt.
Once happy that his head was in the right place, Danny carried on with abandon in his mission. He could feel the bed linen rubbing against the end of his cock. It felt nice and was therefore followed an inkling within his loins; he could tell that he was getting closer to climax. Danny upped his stroke rate to an even more furious pace than before and tried to focus his thoughts more selectively. The undulating bed sheets made a lot of noise and, for the time being, Danny could hear nothing else. His eyes were shut so tightly, and his concentration on the job at hand so intense that he was oblivious to all the sights and sounds around him. Eventually, after another minute or so, he lifted the sheets off the end of his cock with his free hand and finally, having reached the promised land, ejaculated.
Phew! That was hard work!
Danny rested for a moment. With all the exertion, he was out of puff, and his breaths were coming hard and fast. Then, turning his head to the right, he opened his eyes and reached out for the box of tissues on his bedside cabinet. He had to have an astonished double-take when he saw that a cup of tea had been placed there.
Where the fuck did that come from?

Danny instinctively looked toward his bedroom door. To his shock, it was half open. Then his shock turned to horror on seeing that his petite, perm-haired mother (wearing her cleaner's housecoat in readiness for a day of housework) was standing in the opening. Danny closed his eyes and gritted his teeth. Then, there was a feeling of hotness in his cheeks as a bright red blush of extreme embarrassment and anxiousness spread itself all over his face.
'I heard you walking about from downstairs, so I thought I'd bring you up a nice cup of tea,' Danny's mother said. A very tense silence followed until she continued, 'Oh and best stop the... You know...' She nodded towards his groin, 'They say it makes you go blind.' And with those wise words, she exited the room, shutting the door behind her. Danny covered his eyes with his fingers and dragged his open palms slowly down his face in anguish. 'Jesus Christ!' He muttered under his breath.
'AND WHEN YOU GET TO SPAIN DON'T DRINK THE WATER! IT'LL UPSET YOUR TUMMY!' His mother shouted from the landing before descending down the stairs.
Danny just lay there for a while, staring at the ceiling in contemplation. He tried to make sense of recent events.
That didn't happen. Things like that just don't happen. He was a successful estate agent... Successful twenty-year-old estate agents don't get caught wanking by their mums, do they? It must've

been the drugs from the night before. That sulphate must have been too strong, and he'd had a hallucination. Or, maybe it was a bad dream... Everyone has bad dreams now and again.
Then Danny lifted up the bed sheets and peered down at his matted pubic hair and the mess on his belly. Danny was hit with stark realisation and then had to admit to himself that the disastrous situation he found himself in was indeed reality.

...

OVER THREE HOURS had passed before Danny made his way downstairs, dragging his newly packed suitcase behind him. He left the suitcase in the hallway and walked into the lounge. His father was sitting in his usual chair reading the newspaper. Danny sat down on the matching chocolate-brown leather sofa opposite. He tentatively nodded at his mum, who was doing some ironing in the corner of the room. Danny's dad slammed the newspaper into his lap with a loud slap and looked directly into Danny's eyes. Danny knew there was something on his father's mind. Danny couldn't help thinking that his dad had a very stern look on his face, and a rush of nervous anxiety and trepidation shot through him. Danny's dad was a wiry man with a balding head. His sharp facial features and pale olive skin gave away his Jewish origin. There had been much tragedy and hardship in Danny's father's childhood. His family had suffered horribly in the holocaust of World War Two. His parents had met their end in a Polish concentration camp, which meant only Danny's father and his brother had survived. On arrival in the UK from Poland, the two teenage brothers, realising that they'd been given a second chance (and out of respect for their dead parents), never looked back. As soon they could leave school, they got jobs in the building trade. They both worked extremely hard and learned new skills. Then, in the early sixties, when they were both in their thirties, they started their own very successful fitted kitchen business. Danny had worked for his dad for a few months after leaving school, but spending his working day doing hard, physical labour wasn't for him. Eventually, after a couple of boring office admin jobs, Danny decided that he needed something where he could also use some of his natural flair for salesmanship and decided on a career in estate agency instead.

Danny's father's harsh upbringing and self-made rise to successful businessman meant he had no time for losers, and he didn't beat around the bush when telling them so.

'We need to talk.'

Danny took notice that the stern look on his father's face seemed to have intensified. Danny looked over at his mother despairingly with an expression of sheer panic all over his face. *Does he know?*

Danny's mother looked into Danny's terrified eyes and could tell what her son was thinking (as loving

and attentive mothers always can) and shook her head along with a half-smile, reassuring her son that their little secret was safe.
'I've been thinking... You've done well at this estate agency thing...' Danny's father couldn't help noticing the massive sigh of relief that Danny let out. 'You alright son? Is something wrong?'
'No... Sorry Dad, I'm just a bit tired.'
'Yeah, well... Anyway, I've been thinking whether you'd like to run your own office. I could start you off with some money to get things off the ground. So, what do you think?'
'Blimey!' Danny was taken completely by surprise. They'd never discussed any such opportunity before.
'In the newspaper it says there could be a property boom on the horizon. It could be a really good time to start up your own agency.'
'That would be brilliant! I won't let you down dad - I promise.' Danny leapt off the sofa and went over to hug his dad.
Having lost most of his own close family in such tragic circumstances had made Danny's dad very appreciative of the small, loving family he'd now built around him. He was determined that there would be no emotional barriers between him and his only son. He squeezed Danny tightly and kissed him on the cheek. 'Have a think about it while you're on holiday and we'll work it all out when you get back.'

Four

The Kitchen Sink

February 3rd 1972 – Ten years previously...

'SHE LOOKS REALLY peaceful.' Kevin spoke quietly as he and his brother, Steve, sat at the dining room table sipping cups of tea. 'How long has she got? You know... How long before...'

'Maybe today... maybe tomorrow... maybe the day after that... Who knows? All I want is that there's no more pain.'

At the other end of the room, under the large, rounded bay window, was a hospital bed where Steve Hunt's wife, Wendy, was in a state of unconsciousness. Wendy had been administered a hefty dose of morphine by the visiting nurse earlier in the day to make her last moments in this world pain-free and more comfortable.

Wendy had been diagnosed with cervical cancer eighteen months earlier. But, unfortunately, because she'd had no obvious symptoms, it had been caught late, by which time the disease had spread to other parts of her body, and now there was nothing more that could be done to try and save her.

'It's nice you could get Wendy home for her last days.'

'Yeah, the care team and all the doctors and nurses have been great.' Steve paused for thought, 'I still can't get my head around it all.' Steve took a deep breath and then exhaled it slowly as he tried to hold back the tears. 'She's thirty-five mate… How can this happen?' He shook his head disconsolately. 'Just look at her. She's still beautiful even now, and it's not just on the outside, but on the inside too. I'm going to miss that smile that could just melt a person. That infectious laughter. Her sartorial elegance. All that love and kindness. Her wisdom. She was always there for people and would help anyone when the chips were down. It just doesn't seem fair.' Steve hung his head with sadness and despairingly put his hands over his watering eyes.
'She's certainly was a beautiful lady.'
Steve managed to muster a downward, sad smile as he glanced lovingly at his stricken wife. 'Not was… For whatever time is left, she still is Kev.'
'Yeah… Sorry, my mistake.' Kevin decided to make an attempt at taking the gloomy edge off the mood in the room. 'Don't know what she ever saw in a loser like you though,' he joked and, with a smile, gently patted his brother on the cheek in a show of tenderness. 'And, like you just said, it's not fair mate. There's one you did forget to mention though.'
'What did I forget?'
'Her magnificent tits.'
'What did you just say?'

'Phew... Bloody hell… I mean... I know she's your wife and all that, but you couldn't help but admire them. I bet you had some fun with those. The mind boggles.'
'Fucking hell Kev, shut it!' Steve turned to face his brother with a look of disgust. 'What a thing to say! Good thing we're talking quietly... She can still hear you know.'
'Sorry mate, I got carried away. I was just trying to lighten the mood. You know, it's my black sense of humour that took over and all that. I don't do death and dying very well.'
Steve shook his head in dismay, but at the same time found some forgiveness for his outspoken brother. Steve was well used to his brother's strange sense of what was funny and his habit of saying the wrong thing at the wrong time. 'You're such an arsehole sometimes Kev - you really are.'
'Bachelors make good arseholes. It's our prerogative. We don't have anybody else to answer to. Anyway, if I was lying on my death bed with some bird sitting where I'm sitting now and she announced that she thought I had a magnificent cock I'd die a happy man to be honest.' Kevin shrugged his shoulders. 'Wendy would understand.'
Kevin was thirty-seven years old, had never married and was three years his brother's junior. He was the more hard-nosed of the two brothers and seemed to sail through life without a worry or care. Kevin was a serial womaniser and on the borders of being an alcoholic. In his teenage years,

after years of getting into street fights, he'd taken up boxing, which had calmed him down, and he had become a promising talent until women and booze got the better of him. Kevin's crooked, previously broken nose and facial scars were a testament to his fighting and boxing years. He still liked to train at the boxing club between visits to the pub, and the training kept him in surprisingly good shape despite his unruly lifestyle.

In contrast, his elder brother was a gentler soul, which was reflected in his softer features and mildly flabby body. In his adult years he had always found comfort in having a steady girlfriend. Steve was not a risk taker; he had taken a straight and narrow path through life and always looked at things on the cautious side.

There followed a few moments of awkward silence until Kevin spoke to break the ice and, in a caring voice, enquired, 'So, how's young Brian taking it? I mean… You know… Does he realise what's coming?'

Steve let out a heavy sigh, 'I can't bring myself to tell him his mum's going to die. Obviously, he realises that something is very wrong, and I think he knows it's very serious. But, you know how it is Kev, Brian's got issues. He doesn't see things the same way as we do, and I think the way his brain works means he keeps it all inside and well hidden. He bottles it all up. How do you explain to a nine-year-old with learning difficulties that his mother's dying? Sometimes it's hard to know if he's taking

it all in. I just hope, when the time comes, it's not too much for him to bear.'
Kevin felt a sudden rush of compassion, which was unlike him. 'Well… Yeah… It's tough. Look, mate, if there's anything I can do, or if you need a shoulder to cry on… Well… You know where I am.' Feeling uncomfortable with this newfound, strange emotion, Kevin decided it was time to make a move. He got up from his chair, 'Look mate, I've got to shoot. I've got a date with some bird I blagged in the supermarket yesterday. A tidy-looking bit of stuff, even if I do say so myself.'
'Nothing changes with you, does it Kev?'
'Not if I can help it... No.'
Before heading for the door, Kevin walked over to the bed where Wendy was still peaceful. There was another rush of compassion. The finality of what he saw before him got into his head and he didn't know what to say or do. He could feel a tear forming and brusquely brushed it away before Steve noticed it. He leaned over the metal-framed bed and gently kissed Wendy on the forehead. 'See you later sweetheart,' was the best he could do.
Steve walked with his brother out of the front room and into the hallway to see him out of the house. They said their goodbyes, but just as he was closing the door, Steve remembered what his brother had said earlier. 'You know you said if there's anything you can do?'
'So I did.' Kevin turned around looking suspicious and inquisitive at the same time.

'Look, when this is over. You know, when Wendy…' Steve had to stop himself. He shut his eyes with an anguished expression because he couldn't bring himself to say the death word. 'Anyway, will you promise me that if anything happens to me you'll look after Brian?'
'Fuck me mate. That's a bit morbid.'
'I know, but he's happy around you. Everybody else has either gone or lives too far away. I just want to know that there'll be someone there for him if the worst happens.' Steve's mood brightened very slightly as he continued, 'He's found these two buddies at school. They're good boys and they look out for him. You know, they stand up for him and stop him from getting teased or bullied. He's been through enough of that mate. I wouldn't want him to have to start all over again in a strange place, in a new school and go through all the torment again. You know how Brian is, he doesn't communicate very well and he finds it difficult to make friends. But these two kids, Jude and Danny, seem to get the best out of him, and I wouldn't want him to lose that.'
Kevin was uncomfortable with the thought of taking on somebody else's child - even if it was his only brother's. He was just about to tell Steve how he wasn't cut out for looking after children (especially ones with issues like Brian), but Steve pleaded with him before he could utter the words.
'Please, mate, promise me you'll look after him. You don't know how much that would mean to me at the moment.'

Kevin could see the sincerity and hurt in his brother's eyes, and compassion got the better of him one last time. 'Yeah… Of course… No problem. But nothing's going to happen Steve. You're obviously, and understandably, in a bad place at the moment, but I think you're getting things out of perspective.'
'I hope you're right, but when I see my thirty-five-year-old wife lying on her death bed in the next room, it sort of makes you realise your own mortality. Anything can happen Kev.'
Wendy never regained consciousness and passed away in the early hours of the following day.

...

Wednesday 7th July 1982...

THAT WAS ALL ten years ago, and unfortunately for Brian, in this year of 1982 (just as he was on the cusp of his twentieth birthday), his father's words, "*Anything can happen*", had become tragically true. Brian Hunt's dad, Steve, had been killed in a road traffic accident a few months ago in late April.
Steve was a van courier driver and had pulled up in a lay-by on a busy single-track "A" road to check directions for his next drop. A few seconds later, a dumper truck, with a driver who had dozed off at the wheel veered off the road and ploughed into the

back of Steve's Ford Escort van. Steve died instantly as the whiplash effect snapped his neck. Four years before the tragedy, Steve had remarried to Glenda. She had no maternal instinct, no inclination to ever have children of her own, and merely tolerated Brian's existence. Glenda had never shown Brian any particular love or affection. Although Glenda had never been outwardly unkind to him, she felt no bond with Brian. To her, Brian's personality problems and learning issues just made him a bit of a burden. So, after playing the grieving widow for as long as she deemed necessary in honour of Brian's dad's memory, Glenda decided to move her badminton partner and lover (with whom she'd been having a steamy, secret affair for more than a year) into the family home and Brian wasn't part of their plans.

Steve had made a Will and Glenda had insisted at the time that the house was left to her. Brian's inheritance would be a sum of cash that Steve had put aside for him. Steve had expected, at the time of making his Will, that if he was no longer around Glenda would continue to look after his son. However, he had also told Glenda of his pact with Kevin over Brian's future early on in their relationship; long before they'd made any plans to marry. So, as Brian was now just a thorn in Glenda's side with regards to her future happiness and just stood in the way of her new relationship, she decided one early July evening to phone Kevin and remind him of his obligations.

Kevin had never liked Glenda very much. He'd always found her pretentious. He felt she looked down on him due to his womanising and drinking ways and also that she had her head firmly up her own backside. With no love lost between them, Glenda and Kevin's conversation was short and terse:

'Kevin?'
'Yeah...'
'It's Glenda.'
'Hi Glenda, is everything okay?
'No.'
'Why, what's up?'
'It's Brian...'
'What about Brian? What's wrong?'
'He needs to leave. He can't stay here anymore.'
'What do you mean? It's his house.'
'No, it's not his house, it's my house. Steve left it to me, and Brian can't stay here. You promised Steve that you would look after him.'
'Yes, I did. But, look if it's something he's said or done... You Know... He's been through a tough time. He has certain issues Glenda, so sometimes he says and does things he doesn't mean. Maybe you just need to talk to him.'
'It's nothing like that.'
'So, what is it then?'
'Look, I've found someone else Kevin. I'm moving my boyfriend in and Brian just isn't part of our future plans, so he can't stay here.'

‘Fuck me! That didn’t take long, did it? Poor Steve’s hardly cold in his box!’
‘I don’t think you’re in any position to judge me Kevin – not with the way you live.’
‘You were at it before he died, weren’t you?’
‘That’s got nothing to do with you.’
‘I don’t believe this...’
‘Can you come and pick him up tomorrow?’
‘God, you really are in a rush, aren’t you?’
‘There’s no point in prolonging things. It’s just the way it is I’m afraid.’
‘Yeah, I’ll pick him up... Poor kid he’s better off out of there.’
‘What time?’
‘Oh, I don’t know... Make it eleven... Is that okay? Or, will it be interrupting a late morning leg-over with your new man?’
‘There’s no need to be facetious.’
‘Yes there is... There’s every reason to be facetious. Fuck knows what Steve ever saw in you.’
‘I’m tired of this conversation now Kevin.’
‘Yeah, So am I. I’ll be round in the morning’.
‘I’ll have his things ready. Goodbye Kevin.’
‘Oh, before you go Glenda, there’s one last thing...’
‘Yes, what is it?’
‘You’re a cunt!’

The line went dead.

...

BY THE TIME Kevin arrived at the house the next morning, Brian was already standing outside on the front lawn dressed in baggy blue jogging pants and a loose-fitting black T-shirt. By his side was a large suitcase. It had been two months since Kevin had last seen Brian at Steve's funeral and he noticed that Brian had lost weight. At just under six feet tall and noticeably plump, Brian was still a lump. But his face looked gaunt, which made the weight loss much more apparent. His thick, mousey, mid-length hair was untidy and could do with cutting and a wash. Brian just had a kind of lost look about him.

Kevin didn't bother to ring the bell and thus avoided any more contact or conversation with Glenda – last night was the last words they'd ever speak as far as he was concerned. He loaded Brian's heavy, grey, buckled suitcase into the trunk of his Porsche 924, and swiftly after that, they set off.

Brian just stared straight ahead, taking no notice of the route, roads or his surroundings. Kevin had recently moved into a newly built apartment block in Hertford that was quite a distance from Brian's home in North London. Brian didn't ask where they were going because, in his present dark mood, he didn't really care.

Throughout the twenty-minute drive, Kevin tried to make light, jovial conversation with Brian. But, he got back virtually nothing from his nephew, who would only give one-word answers. Brian was too

busy thinking. He didn't understand what was going on in his life or where it was leading him. Why had Glenda kicked him out? Why did his mum have to die? Why did his dad have to die? What had he done that had been so wrong to deserve all this?
Kevin pulled up in the non-descript apartment block's car park. They'd arrived at what was to be Brian's new abode. 'You'll be alright with me mate,' Kevin said while reassuringly patting Brian on the knee. Brian turned toward Kevin and tried to conjure up some sort of smile, but his lips instinctively curled downwards instead of upwards and started to noticeably quiver. Kevin could see Brian's pain and realised he was in a dark place right now.
'Yeah,' Brian said, breaking the eye contact and once again staring straight ahead. He didn't know if he'd be alright; nothing was alright anymore. All that he knew was that shortly he was going on holiday with his two best pals, Jude and Danny - *they'd look after him*. They'd make him laugh, and all three of them would have a brilliant time. And, in the meantime, until Saturday came around (and being as he'd booked an extra few days off from his job stacking shelves at his local supermarket), he was going to just stay in and watch a lot of TV.

...

Saturday 10th July 1982...

THREE DAYS LATER, Brian was sitting on the sofa in the front room of Kevin's apartment watching TV. He was finding it hard to concentrate on what he was watching because of the excitement of his upcoming holiday. Brian's nerves were getting the better of him, and he had butterflies in his stomach. It was Saturday, and the taxi that would take him, Jude and Danny to the airport was due to arrive at midday, which was still fifteen minutes away. He got up and decided to re-check the suitcase that was lying on the sofa next to him. He opened the case and checked it for the umpteenth time. Brian tried to think if there was anything else he would need to take to Spain. The suitcase was still much as Glenda had packed it when she'd decided he was no longer welcome in her house. All that Brian had removed were a few personal belongings, such as his radio clock alarm, a framed photo of his real mum and dad on their wedding day and his Sony Walkman cassette player, which was the last present his dad had bought him before his death. He had considered taking the Walkman, but it meant too much to him, and if it got lost or broken, he'd never forgive himself. Other than that, every item of clothing that Brian possessed was still inside.
Brian hadn't ventured out at all in the last few days since his uncle had come to pick him up, and he still had no idea where he was now actually living.

Kevin wasn't at home that morning. He'd left for his local pub, 'The Bell', at six o'clock the previous evening. Then, after a heavy night's drinking, he'd managed to chat up the new barmaid who was doing her first shift and ended up staying the night at her place.
Kevin was now closer to fifty than forty, but (despite his unforgiving, boozy lifestyle) he still had a reasonably youthful complexion about him and could still easily get away with being mistaken for a man in his late thirties. That being the case, even though he'd only recently moved into the area, this was far from the first liaison with the female staff members at The Bell. There had already been three barmaids previously that had become notches on his bedpost. So much so that the other pub regulars had already given him the nickname *"The Barmaid Banger of The Bell"*.
Kevin had woken up at ten-thirty that morning with a severe hangover, and he wasn't getting out of bed anytime soon. It had been a late night. Kevin and his latest conquest had got back to her place just after closing time. They'd had a few more drinks while listening to a bit of music. After a bit of chit-chat, Kevin had made his move kissing her, and their tongues were rolling around each other's mouths for what seemed like an age. Then, having finally hit the bedroom at around two thirty in the morning they had an hour of foreplay and sex. Kevin's head was banging, but that had never stopped him still feeling horny before. So, instead of feeling sorry for himself, he turned over on his

side and seeing the pretty, thirty-ish barmaid who was still lying next to him, he shifted himself across the bed and got up close. Then, getting busy with his hands and tongue, Kevin decided to work off his hangover in the only way that seemed appropriate right now. And, for the time being, Brian's impending holiday was the last thing on Kevin's mind.

One sensible thing Kevin had done before he'd left for the pub on the Friday evening was to phone Jude and give him the address details for his newly built apartment block. This was because, as the building had only recently been completed, not many of the taxi companies or their drivers were familiar with it.

Being still in a bit of a nervous muddle, Brian decided that he'd better leave a note for his uncle just in case Kevin had forgotten that he was going on holiday. He found a pen and a piece of paper by the telephone. His handwriting wasn't very good, so he decided to write it in capital letters and then scribbled:

UNCLE KEVIN,
I HAVE GONE ON HOLIDAY.
BYE.

The butterflies in his stomach were still getting the better of him and he decided to check his suitcase one more time. After doing so, and just as he was about to close the lid, Brian had a sudden thought about food. Brian had never been abroad before and didn't have a clue about what to expect. He didn't know what Spanish people ate. Did they eat sliced bread? Did they eat cheese? He was particularly concerned about these two food items because, over the last few days, it was all he had eaten, and he had become addicted to cheese sandwiches. *What if there were no cheese shops?* He opened the suitcase lid again and headed into the kitchen. In the fridge, he found a large block of cheddar cheese, and in the bread bin, there was half a loaf of sliced white bread. He took the food essentials, went back into the front room and packed them into his case. He was sure his uncle wouldn't mind. As he closed the suitcase he heard the honking of a car horn from outside the block. He went over to the second-floor window and saw the taxi down below with the driver standing outside, puffing on a cigarette. Before leaving, Brian decided it would be best to add to his note so as to inform Kevin of the missing bread and cheese:

TOOK BREAD AND CHEESE TO EAT.

Brian added thoughtfully.

The driver had decided that Brian would be the first pick-up as the address was off the route to the airport. Brian grabbed his case, walked the few strides to the front door and, just before shutting it behind him, took one more moment of reflection to think carefully about whether there was anything that he might have forgotten. Brian stood in the half-open doorway, and after running it all through his head again, he finally reassured himself he had everything he needed. Brian shut the door behind him. There was still a little trepidation as the door closed and clicked on its latch because Kevin had neglected to issue Brian with a door key yet. *It's too late now,* Brian thought to himself as he headed down the stairwell. He walked out into the car park and approached the waiting taxi. The driver stepped up to Brian and grabbed the handle of his heavy suitcase. The driver let out a groan as he struggled with the unexpected weight and had to grab the case with both hands in order to lift it into the trunk of his taxi.

'Blimey, what you got in there? The kitchen sink?'

Brian didn't have a clue what the taxi driver meant by that, but smiled back politely anyhow.

Five

Getting the Hang of Things

Saturday 10th July 1982...

‘OKAY, SO WHERE are we going?’ Sharon, the lady taxi driver, said cheerily as she turned around from the driver’s seat to face the male customer in the rear seat. She was in a good mood because it’s not often you get an airport job and manage to pick up a fare on the way back as well. It was double bubble and she could do with the money.
‘Home.’ Brian was disconsolate. Things hadn’t turned out well at all.
‘And where might home be?’
‘I don’t know.’
‘You don’t know where you live?’
‘No. Didn’t he tell you?’ Brian was referring to Jude, who had briefly spoken to Sharon through the car window before dashing back into the airport’s terminal building.
‘No, he didn’t. I think he was in a bit of a rush. He was just explaining about the passport thing and that you were a bit...’ She stopped herself in mid-flow, thinking that if she continued, it could cause her paying customer offence.
‘A bit what?’

'A bit...' Sharon still couldn't think of a way to put it gently.
'A bit thick?' Brian said grim-faced.
'Well, yeah... Something like that... And that you're very upset.' Sharon was trying to show empathy for Brian's current predicament.
Brian opened the car door. 'I'll see if I can find Jude.' Before slamming the door shut, Brian got out and poked his head back in. 'He's the only one who knows where I live.'
Sharon let out a heavy sigh. This wasn't going well at all. What she had thought was going to be a positive thing was quickly turning into a negative thing and a bit of a nightmare. It had been a very busy twenty-four-hour period for Sharon. The previous day, after finishing the regular fare-paying runs delivering shoppers to supermarkets around town throughout the day and running school children back to their various addresses in the afternoon, she'd got stuck straight into the Friday evening pub and club runs. She hadn't finished her shift until the early hours of this morning.
Without getting much time for sleep, Sharon had started work again early at eight o'clock in order to catch the Saturday morning shopper's fares.
Therefore, by now (and even though it was still only early afternoon), she was feeling pretty exhausted. Sharon leaned back in the driver's seat, scratched her head and ran her fingers through her shoulder-length, auburn hair. Feeling a little stressed, she closed her eyes for a few moments

and thought about her current situation. *You do get them, don't you?*
The back door of the Ford Cortina swung open again and Brian sat down. 'I couldn't find him.'
Brian had made his way through the terminal building, but amongst the throng of people in the busy, packed airport, he'd quickly realised that there was no chance of finding his friends. Unbeknownst to Brian, they were already past passport control anyway.
Unfortunately, (after all the checking and rechecking) the one thing Brian had neglected to check was to make sure his passport was in the suitcase. It wasn't. So, after a frantic fifteen minutes of searching every nook and cranny of his suitcase (which included tipping the entire contents of his case over the airport terminal floor), Brian realised his dreams of a great holiday in Spain were over. No passport - no holiday.
Jude had come outside with Brian to help him find a taxi back home and had luckily managed to hail down Sharon just as she was departing the drop-off area outside the main terminal building, having just dropped off her passengers. The whole thing had been a rush because the flight to Alicante was already on its last call. Jude didn't have much time and needed to get back into the terminal building and through passport control quickly. In his haste, Jude had forgotten to inform Sharon of Brian's Uncle Kevin's address, and now, being as Brian had never asked or ventured out over the last few days, he had no clue of his intended destination.

'We're not going anywhere then, are we?'
Brian, realising that the situation was looking hopeless, decided to try and explain his predicament further. 'I've only been there a few days. It's my Uncle Kevin's house. I'm only there because my stepmother kicked me out of my old house.'
'Oh, that's terrible. Why did she do that?'
'Because I'm a bit thick, and she doesn't love me I guess.'
Sharon looked at Brian's glum face. She couldn't help taking pity on him and, being the nice person that she was, knew she had to try and get him home. She had a brainwave. 'Okay, so I'm assuming that you know where you used to live? You know where your stepmother's house is?'
Brian nodded.
'Well, let's head there then, and hopefully, she'll be able to tell us where you live now.' Sharon was proud of being able to come up with what she believed was a credible solution. Brian gave Sharon the address in Enfield, North London and they headed off.

...

'YOU'RE LATE,' THE middle-aged, pony-tailed, female flight check-in agent said, peering over the top of her glasses like a schoolteacher and with a look and tone of obvious irritation. Jude and Danny had cut things fine. They'd been delayed by the

lengthy search through Brian's suitcase in an effort to find his missing passport. Then, because Jude had to go back and help Brian find a taxi and his subsequent sprint back to get through passport control meant they'd only just made it to the departure gate with very little time to spare.
'You've been holding everybody up.'
'Sorry, but we had a...'
The agent cut Danny short. 'It's irrelevant now. Where's the other one? There should be three of you.'
'Well, that was the problem you see, he...'
The lady cut Danny short again. 'I'll put out one last call to him and that's it. If he's not here in one minute flat, then the plane flies without him. Now, I've got the surname down here as Mr Hunt...' The lady plonked a finger down pointing at the name on her check-in register. 'But I don't have a first name, so what is it?'
'Well, as I was trying to explain...' Danny was cut short this time by Jude's hand over his mouth.
Jude didn't like the lady's attitude. It was time to have some fun. 'His first name is Watak.'
'Pardon?'
'Watak... his first name is Watak.'
The lady picked up a pen and a scrap piece of paper. 'Spell it for me.'
'W... A... T... A... K.'
'Mmmm... Very odd... In all my years of doing this job I've never come across a Watak.' The smirk on Jude's face was starting to make the stewardess feel slightly unnerved.

'It's an Asian name... His mum's Asian you see? It's a very popular name in that part of the world apparently,' Jude lied reassuringly which seemed to put the lady at ease.
'Oh well... It takes all sorts I suppose.' The lady shrugged. She leaned forward over her desktop, switched on the microphone and made an announcement on the airport's tannoy system.
'THIS IS THE LAST AND FINAL CALL FOR A MISSING PASSENGER ON FLIGHT DA2133 TO ALICANTE WHICH IS ABOUT TO DEPART. WATAK HUNT, MAKE YOUR WAY TO DEPARTURE GATE 9 IMMEDIATELY BECAUSE YOU ARE HOLDING THE FLIGHT UP. I REPEAT... WATAK HUNT'.
The lady looked up from the microphone and was surprised to see the faces on the people around her. Jude and Danny, still standing in front of the check-in desk, were doubled-up with laughter, as were some of the other waiting passengers who were queuing down the gangway. She also noticed a look of shock on some of the other passengers' faces, which she found extremely puzzling.
A male colleague, with a panicked expression, rushed over to explain. He ran his finger along what the stewardess had written on the scrap piece of paper on the desk. *WATAK HUNT*. He whispered into her ear. '*Sounds like* what *a cunt.*'
'Oh my God!' The lady clasped her hands to her blushing cheeks with a look of horror. 'I'm so sorry everybody.' She waved the offending piece of paper in the air. 'It's the way it's written you

see?' She glared at Jude. 'You bastard, I could lose my job!' Then she slapped him across the face.

...

SHARON HEADED DOWN the steep hill that was the last leg of the journey to Brian's stepmother's house and, when she saw the correct door number, parked up outside. Brian got out of the car, rang the doorbell and waited. He rang the doorbell again and waited some more. There was no answer. Brian walked back and, shaking his head, got back into the car.

Sharon's solution wasn't going according to plan, and she was now totally exasperated, 'So what do we do now?'

Brian put his finger to his lips and then scratched his head. He was thinking hard. Suddenly, looking pleased with himself, he said, 'I think I recognised something as we were driving in. I think I might know the way.'

'Excellent'. There was a glimmer of hope. 'Where do I go?'

'Turn around, go to the top of the hill and turn left.'

Sharon duly complied. She turned around and headed up the hill. 'Left down here?'

'Yeah, and then do another left at the end.' It was a short road. 'Now turn right.' They drove for another half-mile. 'Turn right again.'

'For someone who didn't know where they were going, you really seem to be getting the hang of things now.'
'Yeah, it's all coming back to me now.' Brian was feeling pleased with himself. Then, after a short distance, he saw another familiar road. 'Turn right into this road here.'
'Will do.' After a few hundred yards, Sharon recognised the steep hill in front of her and realised they were back where they'd started. 'Oh, for Christ's sake! We're back here again!'
Unfortunately, Brian didn't drive and had no real sense of direction. 'Sorry.' His finger returned to his lips along with a pensive look. 'I'll try the bell again.' He got out of the car and tried the doorbell once more. As before, there was no reply, and he returned to the car.
Although Sharon sympathised with Brian's predicament, she decided there was no other option than to call time on the situation. 'Look, we're not getting anywhere, are we? It's been a long day, I'm tired and I'm hungry.'
'I've got some bread and cheese in my suitcase; I can make you a cheese sandwich if you like.'
Sharon lost patience. 'No, I don't want a bloody cheese sandwich! Just tell me what you want to do!'
'I want to go on holiday.' Brian's eyes started getting teary.
'What?'
'I want to go on holiday.'

'I know you want to go on holiday, but it doesn't...' Noticing Brian's moistening eyes, Sharon's tone softened. 'Look, there's not going to be any holiday I'm afraid. Perhaps we can find you a local...'
Before Sharon could finish Brian interjected. 'We can have a holiday! Me and you! Come with me!' He sounded exuberant and overjoyed at having thought of a fantastic new plan.
'What? What are you talking...'
'I've got some money.' Brian pulled a large wad of notes from his trouser pocket.
'Bloody Hell! How much have you got there?'
'Five thousand pounds.' It was a part of the inheritance he'd been left by his dad.
'What did you bring all that with you for? You were only going on holiday to Benidorm, not trying to buy the place.'
'Sorry, I don't get it.'
She raised a hand, halting the conversation.
'Look... It doesn't matter. What on earth were you going to do with all that?'
'I wanted to have a good time - buy things and stuff. Let's go on holiday... Please? I'll pay for everything. I just want to go on holiday. Come with me.'
A strange feeling of indecision came over Sharon. She couldn't understand why, curiously enough, she was actually considering Brian's offer. She could do with a break - it had been a tough year for her.

Six months previously, Sharon had been in a toxic relationship with an all-controlling boyfriend. If he hadn't been able to control her with words and actions, then he would use his fists instead. While he was at work one day, Sharon had packed her bags, escaped their shared flat in Essex, and moved back to her mum and dad's house. The controlling boyfriend didn't take to that very well, and soon after, he threw a brick through her parent's house's front window. He followed that by making threats against them too. The police were informed. He was charged, found guilty and there was now a court injunction in place ordering him to stay away.

Since leaving her ex-boyfriend, Sharon had worked all hours in her taxi for months trying to raise enough money for a deposit on her own place. She wasn't far off her target now and, if she was honest with herself, pretty much on the brink of exhaustion, all of which made Brian's offer of a free holiday even more tempting.

While taking time to contemplate the prospect, Sharon looked at herself in the car's rearview mirror. Her face was looking chubby. The long days and nights of driving meant her diet had been bad and she'd put on weight. She'd gone from a dress size of twelve to a size fourteen. There'd been too much eating on the hoof and rushing food down between fares. Too many burgers, fried chicken, kebabs and pizzas had made her skin look pasty and pale. There were also dark bags forming under her eyes through lack of sleep. Sharon was only twenty-seven, but the hard work and long hours were starting to make her look older. Sharon classed herself as a bit plain-looking. She wasn't pretty, and she wasn't ugly; she was somewhere in between. This lukewarm acceptance of her overall appearance and lack of self-belief had played a part in her choice of men. Whenever an attractive-looking male came onto her, she always dived in head-long too quickly, and she had consistently made the wrong choices. Therefore, Sharon's impetuous nature meant her heart had been broken more times than she cared to think about. With all her previous history of making rash decisions, and the relationship disasters that followed, it was the most mysterious thing that, at this moment in time (even though this was probably one of the craziest situations she'd ever found herself in), a madcap decision was forming. She turned around and faced Brian again. 'Where would we go?

'Brighton.'

'Why Brighton?'

'Because it's nice.' Brian had fond memories of breaks there with his mum and dad.

Sharon mulled the plan over some more. It was only a relatively short drive and she knew Brighton was full of nice restaurants and bars. The thought of dining well and drinking with all expenses paid became too much to turn down. 'Do you know what? Sod it! I could do with a break. But no funny stuff, right?' She wagged her finger at Brian.

'What's funny stuff?

The innocence of Brian's reply assured Sharon that there was no likelihood of any funny stuff. Then, like a bolt from the blue, another obstacle to the unplanned break hit her all of a sudden. S*he had no clothes to wear other than those she had on.*
'No, sorry, we can't... I haven't got any clothes, and where I live is miles away.'
'I'll buy you a load of new clothes There's really good shops in Brighton. You can have whatever you want.'
All doubt was now dissipating and Sharon was sold. The thought of free food, free drink and a brand new wardrobe at someone else's expense was all too tempting. Sharon had already seen that Brian had more than enough cash to pull it off. It was another madly impetuous decision to be taking a holiday with a complete stranger, but she was willing to give it a go. 'Okay, but just for the weekend.'

...

'WILL YOU AND your good lady wife be requiring a double or a twin room sir?' The stuffy, butler-suited, silver-haired male receptionist at Brighton's Grandest Hotel asked politely.
Brian didn't know how to answer and looked confused.
Sharon confidently took charge of the situation. 'I'm not his wife, and we'll have two singles please.' Sharon watched as the receptionist did a

nonchalant shrug of the shoulders and checked his large, handwritten diary for room availability.
'Yes, we have two singles available. Will sir and madam be requiring breakfast or an evening meal?'
Brian just stared at Sharon blankly. 'Yes, and yes,' Sharon said.
Sharon had asked Brian whether there was any particular hotel he wanted to stay at and he had just said, "T*he best one"*. So, The Grandest Hotel it was.
Driving along the seafront, the prominence and grandeur of the imposing Victorian building was impossible to miss. They took advantage of the valet parking, and Sharon's Ford Cortina was whisked away to the private car park.
With check-in complete, Brian dumped his suitcase in his room. Then, as it was now late afternoon, he and Sharon headed for the shops to buy her some new clothes. With closing time just over an hour away, a whirlwind tour of Miss Selfridge's various departments provided Sharon with dresses, skirts, blouses, shoes, bras, knickers and pyjamas.
Although it had all been Brian's idea, every time she bought something, Sharon felt it only polite to ask Brian's consent whether it was okay to make the purchase. He hadn't questioned any of her spending, had paid up willingly and had been true to his word. Sharon was feeling happier and more at ease by the minute.
After a sumptuous evening meal in the hotel restaurant and a couple of after-dinner drinks, Sharon, her exhaustion finally getting the better of

her, retired to her room. Brian stayed down in the bar for a while, admiring the splendour of his surroundings. For the time being, all his woes were behind him, and he was having a lovely time.
As she undressed, Sharon couldn't help thinking that a day that had started out as a bit of a disaster had now turned out to be a very eventful and pleasant one. She looked at herself in the wall mirror and, with her hand, wobbled the flabby stomach that overhung her black knickers. She definitely needed to do more exercise and firm up. But, after the lovely meal Sharon had eaten earlier, instead of the junk food she'd become accustomed to in her mind her flabby bits felt like healthier flabby bits tonight.
Sharon adorned her new red and green check pyjamas and slipped into bed. Before closing her eyes, she analysed the events of the crazy day she'd had. The complete stranger that she'd decided to take a holiday with had so far been true to his word. Yes, Brian obviously had issues with socialising; he lacked confidence, and he was shy. But, with a little prompting, he could hold down a decent conversation and could be quite witty at times. Sharon surmised that it was Brian's shyness and nervousness around other people that was to blame for him sometimes coming across as inarticulate. Sharon could tell after having spent just one evening with Brian that he was a nice man, and for her (after having just emerged from a controlling relationship with a bad man), it was

quite a nice feeling that she now seemed to be the one in control.
Sharon's eyelids became so heavy that they started to close themselves. But, before sleep came, her thoughts turned to tomorrow and she couldn’t do anything else other than look forward to it. It had been quite a while since she’d last felt like that.

...

SUNDAY MORNING STARTED with a full English breakfast. Then, to work off their overindulgence, Brian and Sharon decided to take a walk along the length of the seafront. It was a lovely day. The sun was shining, and the slight breeze meant that the fluffy, white, cumulus clouds were moving briskly across the bright, blue sky.
On the way back, they stopped off at Brighton Pier. They spent some time in the amusement arcade, and after using up all Brian’s loose change, they headed for the Dodgem cars. After that, it was the helter-skelter and finally, a ride on the waltzers tested the constitution of their stomachs; luckily for both, their breakfasts stayed down. Sharon was feeling the happiest she’d been for a very long time, and Brian was feeling it too.
Leaving the pier, they took a stroll down The Lanes district and found some swanky shops where Brian’s pocket took another bashing as he bought Sharon more shoes, clothes, perfume and trinkets. For Brian, money was an irrelevance - it was just a

means to having an enjoyable holiday - and he was only too happy to be spending it on someone he was starting to really care for.
Lunch was hotdogs and portions of cockles and prawns bought from the food stalls along the seafront, which they ate in the sunshine on the pebbly beach.
Mid-afternoon meant afternoon tea with cream cakes and scones back at the Grandest Hotel, which was a completely new experience for them both. Being amidst all the finery and splendour of the hotel's ornately furnished lounge was wonderful and Sharon told Brian she felt like royalty.
The evening brought another delicious meal in the hotel restaurant. Over dinner, Sharon decided she wanted to know more about Brian's troubled history. Brian opened up. He told her about the teasing and bullying he'd suffered at school. He told her about Jude and Danny and how they'd befriended him and looked out for him ever since. Brian told Sharon about the death of his mother, then the death of his father, and finally about his stepmother's decision, after finding a new man, to kick him out of the house that he'd lived in for the whole of his life.
'You poor thing...' Sharon stood up, and leaning over the dining table, she stroked Brian's cheek and then kissed him on the forehead. 'You've had it tough, haven't you?'
'It's alright... My Uncle Kevin will look after me now.'

Sharon couldn't help noticing that, throughout telling his story, there was a distant look in Brian's eyes, almost like he'd sent the problems, tragedy and hurt he'd suffered to a closed, separate, sealed compartment in his brain. There was no sign of self-pity, just a sort of matter-of-factness about the whole thing. The conclusions Sharon came to were that, after having spent the last two days with Brian, he wasn't stupid or thick in the head. For sure, he didn't come across as the brightest spark in the box, but Sharon could see that life had left Brian behind a bit and that, with some nurturing, he would eventually come out of his shell.

The traits that stood out in Brian were his decency and kindness. Yes, he was a little socially inept (but she told herself that could be fixed) and he was also obviously emotionally scarred. Sharon was overcome with a desire and compulsion to look after this man who was seven years her junior.

It had started out with the mad, crazy set of circumstances that had led to Sharon and Brian's first meeting. Then, for Sharon, it was a crazy decision to go on holiday with someone she knew nothing about. But, for Sharon right now, the craziest thing of the whole weekend was that, when all was said and done, she thought she could be falling in love.

...

'YOU CAN COME in if you want,' Sharon said softly as she and Brian stood outside her open bedroom door. It was just approaching midnight, and they'd both had quite a few drinks at the bar after dinner.
'I'm a bit tired,' Brian yawned.
'Look, just come in will you?' Sharon grabbed Brian by the shirt collar and dragged him into her bedroom.
'What do you want?' Brian found himself standing at the foot of her bed.
'I want to make love to you.'
'Oh... Right... Why?' The scenario was all new to Brian; he'd never been in a situation like this before.
'Because I like you.'
Sharon started to unbutton Brian's blue shirt and then pushed it over his shoulders and down each arm. She took comfort in the fact that Brian had flabby bits too. She noticed the uncomfortable look in Brian's eyes. 'You've never done this before have you?'
'No.'
'Don't worry... Relax, I'm in charge okay?'
'Okay.'
Sharon pushed Brian backwards onto the bed. Then, before doing anything else, she stripped off herself.
Now naked, Sharon knelt on the end of the bed. She removed Brian's newly acquired black brogue shoes and pulled off his socks. Next, she unbuttoned Brian's black polyester trousers,

unzipped the fly and slid them down his legs. Brian's brief-style underpants were now very noticeably stretched upwards in the shape of a wigwam, which told Sharon he was ready for action. She started dragging the underpants down, and as they pulled over Brian's fully erect cock it sprang back onto his stomach like there was a strong, elastic band attached to it that had just broken. Sharon was impressed with the size and force of Brian's erection. 'You're big aren't you?'
'Am I?'
'Yes, you are.' Sharon got onto the bed and lay down beside Brian. She wrapped her hand around his cock and caressed it gently.
The new sensation was all too much for Brian. Years of pent-up frustration meant he was unable to control himself, and it only took a few seconds before Brian prematurely shot his load.
Sharon watched in awe as Brian's ejaculation sent what looked like fountain after fountain of white liquid towards the ceiling. It seemed to reach an incredible height before landing on his midriff.
'My God...' She said with incredulity at the ferocity of Brian's orgasm, 'I've never seen anyone explode like that before.'
'Sorry. That's not supposed to happen is it?'
'It's okay, we can fix that. It's all about getting the hang of things. We'll give it half an hour and then we'll try again. Just remember, I'm in control, okay?'
'Okay... You're in control... No problem.'

...

AT THE SECOND attempt at sex, Sharon got on top, and Brian lasted about thirty seconds. They did it again in the morning before breakfast, and Brian lasted just over a minute.

Brian and Sharon made a joint decision at breakfast that, as they were both having such a great time, they'd stay in Brighton for the rest of the week. They changed their single rooms at the Grandest Hotel to one double, which was a better representation of the proper, loving couple they had become. Sharon was, for once, in control of her own destiny. She continued with her efforts to bring Brian out of his shell and to teach Brian all she knew in the bedroom. Throughout the rest of their week in Brighton, Brian's personality revealed itself more and more, and the sex just got better and better.

Six

A Dog with Big Teeth

Friday Night July 16th 1982...

'MY FUCKING BUM'S on fire!' Lyndsey screamed from the bathroom of her Benidorm hotel room. She was bent over double and completely naked in the bath. She was using one hand against the tiled wall for support and the other hand was holding the shower head, with the cold water tap turned fully on, firmly against her painful anus. Through the fiery pain, she turned her nearly watering eyes toward Danny. 'You fucking idiot!'

'Sorry,' Danny said sheepishly. He was standing outside the bathroom with Jude. They, too, were both completely naked. For them, it was a kind of surreal moment in both their lives. Little did they know that the image of Lyndsey with a shower head firmly planted on her backside would be the last and everlasting memory of their threesome encounter. 'Should I call an ambulance?'

'Oh yeah? That would be good. How the fucking hell am I going to explain this? You fucking idiot Danny!'

'Perhaps you could rub some cream in it?'

'Yeah, as if I'd trust you with any more bottles when you don't even read the labels.'

'It was dark.'
'There's a fucking light switch there!' Lyndsey nodded toward the corded light switch that hung from the ceiling.
'Sorry, I couldn't find it..'
Jude, in an effort to calm the situation, walked into the bathroom and, spotting a tube of Aloe Vera gel, he picked it up from the shelf above the sink. 'How about this? Aloe Vera's good for that sort of thing.'
Lyndsey, dropping the shower head, outstretched an arm. 'Give it here.'
Jude handed over the tube and watched as Lyndsey squeezed out a large handful of the gel, rubbed it into her burning bottom and then returned the shower head to its position firmly against her painful behind.
'There is a bright side to all this when it's over Lyndsey.'
'Oh yeah? And what could that possibly be?'
'At least you'll have the cleanest bum in Benidorm.'

…

EARLIER, ON THIS warm Friday evening in Benidorm, events had started out well. There was a good, lively atmosphere in The Beach Rock Bar and Lyndsey had met up (for a last night of drinks and frivolity) with the girlfriends that she'd met in her hotel's bar. It was the final night of Lyndsey's holiday.

Coming away on her own had been a daunting prospect for Lyndsey at first, but she desperately needed a break. On the flight from Manchester she'd been apprehensive. Then, by the time the plane landed at Alicante, Lyndsey had convinced herself that, although she was naturally quite shy, with her amiable personality, she'd soon find someone to talk to and hang out with. Unusually, by the time Lyndsey had checked into her hotel she was full of confidence.

The group of twelve women (of varying ages) that Lyndsey had met in the hotel bar and teamed up with were on a hen week and partying hard. Being fellow Mancunians, the group were only too pleased to take Lyndsey under their cumulative wing.

The Beach Rock Bar had become the group's watering hole of choice. It was a busy bar with a musical theme and a good ambience. The walls were adorned with pictures of famous musical artists dating back from the sixties to the present day. The venue also hosted live bands and had a small dance floor. The Beach Rock was where, three evenings previously, on the Tuesday, Lyndsey had first come across Jude and Danny…

…

Three nights previously…

IT WAS CLOSING in on nine o'clock in the evening. Jude and Danny, finding it hard not to notice the loud conversation and laughter of the large gathering of making-merry ladies further along the bar, had made a beeline for the group of females.
Unfortunately, the two boys weren't the only males in the busy Beach Rock Bar who were attracted to the ladies and competition for partying; female attention was fierce.
After twenty minutes, Danny found he wasn't having much luck at all because the constant distraction from the other men on the scene, combined with the volume of the music, was making any meaningful communication difficult. Jude was having similar problems, but he noticed that there was one girl hanging around on the fringes of the group and slightly further away from the bar's loud, booming speakers who was consistently making eye contact with him. He made a decision to shuffle over as inconspicuously as he could to where she was standing. Then, Danny spotting the sly move out of the corner of his eye and, not wanting to be left out and alone, duly followed.
The first thing that had struck Lyndsey was Jude's piercing blue eyes. She'd never seen that in a black man before. His well-toned chest, broad shoulders and muscular arms, which were accentuated by the

strobe lighting that was bouncing off his coffee-coloured skin, were also a major attraction. Lyndsey had never made out with a man of an ethnic origin before. This wasn't because she felt any prejudice or apprehension towards boys from different cultures - it was purely down to the fact that her father would definitely not approve. Her dad Terry, referred to all those who had a slightly darker skin than him as "Darkies". To Terry (even though being a hardened criminal, he'd contributed very little to society himself), the influx of Darkies, which had started in the fifties and sixties, was to blame for the majority of society's current woes. However, Lyndsey's dad wasn't here; she was on holiday, and the thought of doing something that he would disapprove of made it all the more exciting. There was also the fact that having been sex starved for weeks on end (due to her ex-boyfriend Sebastian's drugs and drink-induced impotence), Lyndsey was feeling sexually unfulfilled and decided she wanted that sexual fulfilment to come in the form of Jude. She didn't want a relationship; she'd had enough of those for the time being - just raw sex with no ties would do for now.
There was an obvious attraction and rapport between Lyndsey and Jude, which meant Danny found himself more or less excluded from the chitter-chatter. After about an hour, Danny needed a piss and headed for the toilet. While he was gone, Lyndsey, realising that if she wanted to have Jude to herself, she would have to find a way of separating the two friends, made her move.

'You know your mate?'
'Yeah...'
'He's a bit boring isn't he?'
'Well, he's....'
Lyndsey interjected before Jude could come to Danny's defence, 'Why don't you and me go somewhere else?'
'Such as?'
'Somewhere we can fuck.'
Jude was taken aback by the brazen remark and, for a split second, was lost for words. However, never being one to look a gift horse in the mouth, he very quickly regained his power of speech and tried to keep his cool. Jude attempted to sound as blasé about the whole thing as he could. 'Yeah... Yeah... Of course. Our apartment block isn't far from here. I'll tell Danny he'll have to amuse himself for the rest of the night.'
On Danny's return, Jude took him aside and explained the situation. Danny wasn't best pleased.
'Oh yeah, and what the fuck am I supposed to do for the rest of the night?'
'You can stay here or go on a crawl. There are plenty of other bars to choose from.'
'I'll look like some lonely fucking saddo.'
'I'm sure you'll find someone to talk to. Look, mate, I've got to go because I'm finding it hard to stand here without getting a hard-on, and I don't want to peak too soon. Try to find yourself a decent-looking bird, and don't get off with any dodgy-looking dogs, okay?' Jude gave Danny a reassuring pat on the back. Then, signalling to

Lyndsey that it was time to depart, the two of them exited the Beach Rock hand-in-hand.

...

'FANCY A DRINK?' Jude and Danny hadn't gone to the trouble of stocking their apartment with a huge amount of booze. They'd decided on buying a small selection of alcohol that they could use for a few early evening warmer-uppers before going out to the bars. Therefore, Jude was slightly embarrassed about the limited choice of drinks he could offer Lyndsey. 'I've got some beer, or I can do you a glass of white wine.'

'I don't want a drink, I just want to fuck.' Lyndsey pecked Jude on the lips and walked across the room past the small, low table that was strewn with empty beer bottles. She noticed the sofa bed and wooden armchair had become resting places for items of unwanted clothing. She slid open the glass balcony doors. She stepped out onto the balcony and took in the view from the high-rise apartment block. As it was situated just a few metres from the beach, the soft sound of the lapping sea gave the atmosphere a romantic touch. If she turned her head to the left, she could see the contrasting, bright, neon lights of Benidorm's bars and restaurants.

'Fuck it is then.' Jude forgot about drinks and slinked up behind Lyndsey, who was still bending forward over the balcony rails, taking in the sights.

He lifted her short, pink skirt above her hips. Then after sliding her red panties down to her ankles, he placed his right hand between her legs and inserted his middle finger into the warmth of her vagina. He could feel that Lyndsey was already very moist.
So, without wasting any more time, he dropped his denim shorts and slid into her from behind. He started off thrusting slowly, and then, with his growing excitement and Lyndsey's soft moans, his thrusts became harder and faster. It wasn't long before Jude was ready to shoot his load and he thought it best you ask whether Lyndsey had taken precautions, 'Are you on the pill?'
'Come in me! Come in me!' Jude took that as an affirmative, and hearing the words almost immediately brought Jude to a crescendo, and very quickly, he spurted with an audible groan.

...

AFTER HALF AN hour of chat and a drink on the balcony, Jude and Lyndsey went into the bedroom and went at it again, this time in missionary position. Then, after another hour of cuddling up to one another with a bit of pillow talk, and as it was now the early hours of the morning, Lyndsey decided maybe it was time to leave.
Lyndsey put her clothes on, and Jude walked her to her door in his still-naked state. He opened the door, but before departing, Lyndsey looked down and saw that Jude's cock was fully erect again. So,

deciding that the erection shouldn't be wasted, she hastily pushed the door shut. Lyndsey stripped off once more and then, with obvious intent, pushed Jude down onto the sofa. They started having sex again, this time with her on top.
Being the third time around, Jude wasn't going to climax any time soon, and after a long spell of exuberant man-riding, Lyndsey was getting out of breath.
'Bloody hell, I'm knackered!' She sank backwards into the sofa, took the weight onto her knees and with her backside high in the air and took Jude's cock into her mouth. Jude closed his eyes, put his hands behind his head and thought, does life get any better than this? All of a sudden, the front door of the apartment flew open...

...

THE FIRST THING that Danny saw was the light-pink-coloured inner cheeks of Lyndsey's over-extended rear-end poking up over the arm of the sofa. Then he noticed her bobbed, peroxide, blonde-haired head rising and falling from Jude's groin, and it momentarily distracted him from his immediate dilemma. Danny wanted to shout, but being very drunk and with the debauched sight before him, all he could manage was a weak-sounding, high-pitched shriek. 'Help!'
Jude, eyes closed and busy with his visions of ecstasy, wouldn't have heard a thing had it not

been for the sound of the violently swinging door opening and thwacking against the wall. He looked up and saw Danny covered in sand. Danny had one training shoe missing, the tails of his red polo-neck T-shirt seemed to have been ripped into strands, his ordinarily neat hair was flung in all directions and there was an expression of sheer panic etched on his face.

'What the...' Lyndsey disengaged and, for the sake of a bit of modesty, frantically started gathering her clothes together that were scattered around the floor.

'I've been attacked!'

'Attacked! Attacked by who?'

'By a dog.'

'By a dog? What was the last thing I said to you? Don't get off with any dodgy-looking dogs.'

'Not a woman dog... A dog... A dog with big teeth dog!'

'Eh?'

'I was heading back and decided to walk along the beach and the fucking thing started chasing me. That's when this happened,' Danny lifted his torn shirt tails. 'I managed to get away and get into the foyer. The fucking vicious bastard's still down there outside reception.'

There was an angry, furrow-browed look on Danny's face (which meant his long, thick eyebrows met in the middle), and Jude recognised the tight-lipped facial expression that Danny always pulled when he was genuinely agitated. Jude decided the situation needed further investigation. He leapt off the sofa and pulled on his shorts, ‘I’ve got to see this.’

...

CATCHING THE LIFT down to the reception area, the two boys headed outside onto the large stone steps while Lyndsey decided to stay in the foyer. Jude scrutinised the surrounding area, but there was no sign of any vicious dog. He took the five large steps down to ground level, and after a few metres, he was on the promenade. Still, there was no sign of a dog. He headed down onto the dimly lit beach.

Danny was too frightened to move off the steps and stayed where he was. ‘Be careful down there, that fucking thing’s a killer!’

Suddenly, Jude caught sight of a fast-moving object approaching him. Danny, with a better view from the safety of the well-lit steps, saw it too and immediately knew it was his attacker.

‘WATCH OUT! THE FUCKING BEAST’S COMING!’

Jude had to think quickly. He decided not to run and instead was determined to show no fear. Then, as he could see the animal closing in on him, he sank to his knees, thinking that a smaller-looking target might make the dog feel less intimidated and also less aggressive. A second later, the dog was upon him. The force of the dog's chest crashing into Jude’s torso, with its head right next to his

inviting neck, caused Jude to fall backwards into the sand. He could do nothing now except accept his fate.
Danny watched but was too scared to make any move and go to the aid of his friend. He turned back toward the open glass doors of the reception area. 'CALL THE POLICE, THERE'S A MAD FUCKING DOG ATTACKING MY MATE!'
The young male Spanish receptionist came rushing out in panic. 'Is there a problem?'
'THERE! THERE!' Danny pointed to the ongoing scene on the beach. 'THAT FUCKING DOG'S EATING MY MATE!'
'DANNY!' Jude shouted from his stricken position on the beach.
'IT'S ALRIGHT THE POLICE ARE COMING!'
There was a worrying silence until Danny thought he could hear Jude laughing. He cupped his ear in his hand to try and catch more sound waves. It still sounded like Jude's laughter.
'HE'S A FUCKING PUSSYCAT!'
'WHAT?'
'THE DOG, HE'S A FUCKING PUSSYCAT. HE'S NOT VICIOUS AT ALL. HE'S LICKING MY FACE!'
Danny stepped down onto the promenade to get a closer look and saw that the dog was, indeed, extremely friendly.
'Hello boy, you're just a pussycat, aren't you?' Jude said while stroking the dog's head and playing with his floppy ears. Jude got to his feet and started strolling towards the promenade.

'Don't you bring that fucking beast near me!' Danny started walking backwards tentatively.
'He was probably just playing - he just wanted to be your friend.'
'Playing!' Danny ripped his decimated, torn shirt over his head in anger and threw it towards the dog. 'If he was just fucking playing and wants to be my friend he can buy me a new fucking shirt!' Then he slid off his one remaining trainer and threw that as well. 'And some new fucking trainers too!'
'Come on boy.' Jude beckoned the dog, led it over to the apartment block, and then, sitting down on the bottom step, affectionately started to stroke and cuddle the animal. 'You rascal. Fancy chasing and scaring my mate like that... He doesn't like you now.'
Jude could see the mainly black-coloured dog, with a splash of white in the middle of his chest and another that led down from the top of his head to his nose was very thin. This accentuated its long muzzle, powerful-looking chest, narrow rear quarter and muscular hind legs. It was not wearing a collar and looked bedraggled and uncared for. Jude guessed the dog was some kind of greyhound or whippet derivative. 'I think we need to get you some food, you rascal. Hey boy, that can be your new name - Rascal.'
The receptionist re-emerged from inside the building, 'Is everything okay now?' Looking down to the bottom step and seeing Jude with his

newfound canine friend, he could see it was. 'They call them Galgos.'
'Sorry?'
'They call them Galgos. They are a hunting dog. People out in the countryside use them for hunting, and when they don't do well or get slow...' He slid his forefinger across his throat in a cut-throat gesture.
Jude wanted to know more. 'What do you mean?'
'They kill them.'
'Bastards!'
'The lucky ones... Sorry, I don't know the word...' The Spanish man was struggling with the proper terminology. 'The hunters they throw them away onto the street and... I'm sorry I forget the word in English...'
Jude helped the receptionist out. 'Abandon?'
'Yes, abandon'. The receptionist nodded in the direction of the dog, 'He is maybe one of the lucky ones and someone has just left him to be wild. Maybe his owner has a little heart and throw him out on the street nearby. Here in Benidorm, he can eat wasted food from the bins and streets until the police find him. But, the police don't want wild dogs on the streets and if they catch him...' He repeated the cut-throat gesture once more.
'We're going to have to look after you then, aren't we Rascal?' Jude looked toward Danny. 'Go and get him some of that salami and cheese we've got in the fridge.'
'Fuck off!'

'Just do it will you? There's some old bread up there too.'
Danny, bare-footed and shirtless, begrudgingly headed back to the apartment to collect the food. Although the dog had given him a fright, he wouldn't forget it for a while. Even Danny couldn't help being a little touched by the Galgo's pitiful plight.

...

Friday night 16th continued...

BEING AS IT was the last night of her holiday, Lyndsey planned to do something different, something she'd never done before, something memorable, something naughty. She'd come up with the plan earlier in the evening and had gotten excited just thinking about it, and now it was time to see if she could make it all come to fruition.
It was now coming up for the midnight hour at the Beach Rock, and Lyndsey was by now quite drunk. She was sitting at a high table canoodling with Jude. Danny was at the table too and, for some reason, the other two didn't know about, looking very sorry for himself. He'd been uncommunicative all evening. Lyndsey could only guess that Danny's subdued moodiness was maybe because he felt left out of things. It was probably due to her and Jude's sexual liaisons that had been happening for the last few days. But Lyndsey's

new plan would put paid to that because Danny was included this time.
Lyndsey whispered into Jude's ear, 'You know your mate?'
'I think I know what you're going to say Lyndsey. You're going to say he's a bit boring.'
'No, I wasn't going to say that actually.' Lyndsey took a deep breath before continuing; it was make-or-break time. 'Do you think he might want to...You know... Join in.'
'He is joining in...' Jude nodded in the direction of Danny, who was still staring into his glass in a world of his own, 'He's sitting just there.'
'That's not what I mean. I meant sexually.' She sighed deeply before continuing. 'Do you think he'd like to fuck me too?'
Jude leaned back bolt upright in his chair with a shocked expression. 'Bloody hell!' He spoke loudly and thus pricked Danny's attention.
'What's going on?'
Jude raised the palm of his hand, halting Danny in his tracks. 'Nothing mate. Well, there is... I'll tell you in a minute, okay?' Danny looked confused.
Jude leaned forward again and went into whispering mode once more. 'Are you blowing me out? Do you want to fuck Danny instead?'
'No, I want to fuck both of you... Together.'
'A threesome?'
'Yeah, a threesome.'
Jude shot back in his chair again, a wild smile on his face. He turned to face Danny once more. 'She

wants a threesome!' He said it loudly enough for a group of four young lads at the next table to hear. One piped up. 'Sounds like fun. Can we join in? Make it a sevensome?' He and his three friends burst out laughing.
Lyndsey cupped her face in her hands, which was red with embarrassment. 'Drink up, we're going,' she said forcefully.

...

OUTSIDE THE BEACH Rock, Rascal was waiting obediently. Jude had taken the dog under his wing. He'd bought a collar for Rascal with his new name on it to make it look like the dog had a home and stop it from being picked up by the authorities as a stray. As the three of them strolled in the direction of Lyndsey's hotel Rascal followed. The dog and Jude had now become constant companions.
On the journey Danny started to have feelings of doubt. He'd gone at the drink and sulphate hard the night before. Thursday night had been a disaster, and Danny had got very little sleep. He was tired, and he wasn't sure he fancied Lyndsey or felt like sex, anyway. He relayed his thoughts to Jude, who pleaded with him to carry on.
'Fucking hell mate, don't let me down... This is a once in a lifetime.'
Reluctantly, Danny carried on walking and decided he'd go through with it for his friend. Danny sort of knew that he should be more up for it. But, the

previous evening's events had shaken him up badly and were the reason why he couldn't feel any excitement about the whole thing.

...

'STAY THERE BOY', Jude instructed Rascal outside Lyndsey's hotel and the dog, knowing his place, went and curled up under a tree in the hotel's plush garden.
Lyndsey led the two boys through the reception area. The middle-aged male receptionist lowered his glasses and looked on suspiciously as the three of them passed his desk. Lyndsey marched on with confidence.
'Hola,' she said cheerily, which seemed to relax the receptionist's suspicions, and they continued up to Lyndsey's room.
As they entered the bedroom, which was decorated and furnished in a typically 1970s style, Jude was already stripping off his clothing. Lyndsey soon reciprocated. But Danny was still showing reluctance. Lyndsey was eager to get going.
'Come on... What are you waiting for?'
Danny lifted his white T-shirt over his head. 'How are we going to do this then?'
'Well, how about we try a spit-roast type of thing. One of us starts at the front with Lyndsey sucking and one at the back fucking. We can swap positions after a while.' Jude was well up for it and looked

over at Lyndsey for any apparent signs of agreement.
'Sounds okay to me,' Lyndsey nodded her approval.
'If I'm going to do this, I want to do it up the arse.' Danny's comment filled the room with a momentary stunned silence.
Jude turned, looked at Lyndsey and raised his eyebrows inquisitively.
It was something Lyndsey had never tried before, but she was the last night of her holiday, and the point was to do new and exciting things. 'I'll try anything once.'

...

THEY STARTED WITH Danny at the front because his erection wasn't full-on and he needed some extra stimulation, which Lyndsey was providing with her mouth. Jude, requiring no extra encouragement, was already pounding into her vagina from behind.
After a couple of minutes, the two boys swapped places. One thing Lyndsey had insisted on is that if they were going anal, Danny would need to use a condom and the agreement was struck. Danny slipped on the condom that Lyndsey had provided and prepared to enter her anus. He pulled her buttocks apart and forced his way into the narrow orifice. It was tight – really tight.

Being a little apprehensive of this newfound experience, Lyndsey was a little uptight and told herself to relax a bit. She was actually enjoying the sensation, but the pain of her stretched anus was a bit too harsh. After a minute, Lyndsey suggested a new approach. 'I think we're going to need some lube. There's some coconut oil in the bathroom.'
'Okay, I'll go and get it.' Danny withdrew and headed off to the bathroom.
Jude could feel he wasn't far off shooting his load and he didn't want Lyndsey to be distracted. 'Don't stop... Keep going.' Lyndsey duly obliged and carried sucking on Jude's cock.
In the bathroom, Danny fumbled his fingers up and down the wall but couldn't locate the light switch. To keep in the moment, he gave up searching after a few seconds and took his chances with the lack of light. He could just make out some bottles and tubes on the shelf above the sink. With squinted eyes, he looked for a substance with suitable lubricant qualities. Danny spotted a bottle of what looked like a thick, transparent liquid that could be the right stuff, but he couldn't make out the writing on the label in the bad light. He decided to take his chances, grabbed the bottle and rushed back to the bedroom.
Danny squeezed the plastic bottle and applied a generous amount of the gloopy lotion to the length of his condom-clad manhood and another generous helping to Lyndsey's anus. Then, wanting to get on with things while his erection was still full-on, he discarded the bottle by throwing it down on the

bed. He re-entered Lyndsey's bottom, and indeed, the movement was far more manageable and less intense now.
A short while later, Lyndsey, still with Jude's cock in her mouth, started to groan loudly. Then she began to writhe from side to side and then forwards and backwards as if trying to get away.
'It's going to hurt a bit, even with the lube,' Danny tried to reassure her.
Jude was about to come, but just at the wrong moment, Lyndsey pulled her mouth away and spoke over her shoulder in Danny's direction.
'It's burning... My arse is burning!' As she spoke, Jude was unable to stop the momentum of his climax, and, being that Lyndsey's head was still turned, all he could do was shoot his load into her left ear.
Lyndsey was now in quite a bit of distress and couldn't understand why. Then she spotted the plastic bottle that Danny had thrown down on the bed beside her and immediately recognised it for what it was.
'You fucking idiot Danny!' Lyndsey leapt from the bed and ran to the bathroom. 'That's my bloody nail polish remover!' Grabbing the shower from its hook on the wall, she turned the cold tap on full, jumped into the bathtub, and pressed the shower head against her burning behind.
'MY FUCKING BUM'S ON FIRE!'

...

THE NEXT AFTERNOON, at one o'clock, Jude and Danny were sitting outside the Beach Rock Bar with their suitcases. It was Saturday - departure day - and getting close to the time when they'd be flying back to England. Because they'd had to vacate their apartment by ten o'clock in the morning, the boys were just killing time until the coach came to take them to Alicante airport. Rascal was lying down by Jude's feet. Jude saw the group that were Lyndsey's girlfriends walking along the promenade in their beachwear and heading towards him, but Lyndsey wasn't with them.

'Hey, where's Lyndsey?'

One of the older ladies looked towards him with a surprised expression. 'Lyndsey?'

'Yeah, Lyndsey... She's here with you lot.'

'Oh, Lyndsey... No, she's not here with us... She came out here on her own. She flew home this morning.'

'She's gone?'

'Yeah, gone...' The lady flapped her arms like a bird, 'Flown mate.' Then, she turned away and walked on, rejoining her friends.

Jude turned to Danny; his tone had a distinct element of disappointment. 'That's that then? That's the end of Lyndsey. You'd think she would've told us. You know... Said goodbye.'

Danny just shrugged his shoulders with disinterest – he didn't really care - and, without saying a word, took a large swig of his beer. Danny had far weightier things on his mind than Lyndsey's unannounced departure.

Seven

Just A Little Drink

Thursday Night 15th July 1982...

DANNY SAT HIMSELF down at a small, round table at the end of the street. He was lucky to get a table at all as the tapas area of Benidorm Old Town was extremely busy.
Jude's night-time sexual liaisons with Lyndsey, which had been going on for the last few nights, meant that Danny had become used to spending the latter part of the evenings on his own. He'd bought himself three small tapas plates from one of the plethora of takeaways that lined the streets in this part of town. The Old Town had become a regular venue for a late-night snack and a last-knocking drink in one of the bars in the adjacent square.
Danny tucked into his plates of chorizo cooked in wine, cheese croquets and cured ham on crusty, white bread while taking in the atmosphere of the crowded area.
Amongst the traditional Spanish bars and British pubs, the square was also home to the gay and transvestite scene in Benidorm. Danny was fascinated by the vibrancy, the outlandish costumes of some of the drag queens who hopped from one

venue to another, and how relaxed everybody out and about was with the whole thing.
Danny continued to study the throng of gay and straight revellers in front of him and he couldn't help thinking that the gay crowd looked like they were the ones having the most fun. From the British pub across the street, he could hear the familiar sound of football-shirt-clad Brits belting out their favourite team's tribal chants. Danny had no interest in football, or almost any other sport for that matter. He had taken an interest in table tennis in his early teens, but with the lack of places to play locally, his enthusiasm soon fizzled out. So, the British pub was out of the question for a last evening drink. The alcohol-fuelled, loud, testosterone-filled ambience wasn't for him and he'd just feel uncomfortable. On previous evenings, he'd ended up trying out some of the quieter Spanish bars, but being all on his own, he'd felt awkward and out of place.
As he was on the last couple of days of his holiday, earlier in the evening, Danny had decided to start using up the sulphate he'd brought from home. He'd hidden it in the lining of his suitcase on the flight out. Danny had taken more of the drug than he usually did and was now speeding out of his brain. He'd almost done the whole packet, and out of the entire gram, Danny estimated there were only a couple of small dabs left at most. He could feel his eyes bulging like they were about to pop out of their sockets. Even though he was wearing a loose-fitting, button-up blue shirt, Danny was

perspiring a lot. There were dark sweat patches under his armpits and more dotted around his torso. His white cotton shorts were clinging to his thighs. On his way to the old town, Danny had stopped off at a busy British bar. On hearing a crowd of lads with familiar London accents laughing and joking, Danny, in an effort to make some new friends and join in the banter, butted in on their conversation. In Danny's speeding brain, he was lucid and coherent. But, the truth was, he was randomly switching from one subject matter to another. He was telling bad jokes, mainly talking nonsense, and everything that came into his muddled head he relayed to the group. Unfortunately, Danny's fellow Londoners weren't on the same wavelength of speed-induced, high excitement and found Danny's constant nondescript conversation (which was delivered at such a pace that anybody else was finding it hard to get a word in) too much to take. 'Look mate, can you just fuck off. You're talking bollocks and getting on everyone's tits,' one of the bigger and more outspoken of the lads told Danny. So, even though he was out of his head, Danny could still comprehend what was a very unsubtle hint. Because of his current state, for a split second, Danny had been tempted to throw a punch at the guy. But he wasn't a fighter, and finding a momentary dash of common sense within him, Danny just turned his head and carried on his way. Danny finished eating the last of his tapas and gulped down what was left of his beer. The drugs he'd taken caused a constant thirst and dryness in his mouth. Danny had lost count of how many beers he’d drunk hours ago, and the copious amounts of alcohol just heightened the confusion in his head. Taking out the moisturiser he always carried from his shorts pocket, Danny massaged a small amount into his dry lips, and while doing so, he made a decision.

...

DANNY FELT A tap on his shoulder and turned around on his barstool to see the grinning form of Pablo behind him.

‘What are you doing here?’ Pablo was a Spanish barman. He worked behind the bar at the Beach Rock. Over the last few days he’d served Danny with drinks many times. Tonight was Pablo’s night off and he’d headed out to one of his regular haunts. ‘I didn’t know you liked this kind of thing.’ Even though he was sitting on a stool in a glitzy gay bar, the question still took Danny slightly by surprise, and he hesitated before giving an answer.

‘I don’t... Definitely not.’

Danny had never thought of Pablo as gay. He didn’t particularly look gay and had always seemed very flirty with the girls who frequented the Beach Rock. He was dressed in everyday clothes - dark blue jeans and a snug-fitting, yellow T-shirt - nothing like the outlandish outfits of some other gay men in the bar. Pablo was quite a big, fit-looking guy. Probably in his late twenties to early thirties, Danny guessed. But, it was hard to tell due to Pablo's short, crop-haired, almost shaven head, his contrasting thick, black moustache and his wiry chin-beard, which perhaps made him look that bit older than he really was.

Pablo spread his arms in amazement, 'Then why are you here?'

Danny hesitated. 'I was... I was just curious.' Starting to feel uncomfortable and to avoid being questioned further, he fired back. 'It's funny... I didn't have you down as an arse-bandit.

'A bandit?' Pablo looked puzzled.

'Yeah, a poof. A bender. A brown hatter. A shit stabber. An anal assassin.' The sulphate was still affecting Danny's ability to think before he spoke and from saying every thought that came into his head. Danny didn't care as to how offensive or shocking his words might come across.

'I'm sorry, I don't understand.'

'Oh, for fuck's sake... Are you a fucking poof?' The speed just increased Danny's irritation. Seeing that Pablo still looked confused, Danny decided that maybe Pablo's English wasn't as good as he had thought. Perhaps the words Danny had used weren't in the Spanish gay community's vocabulary. Danny rephrased the question, 'Are you gay?'

Pablo, now understanding, rocked his head from side to side and looked pensive while thinking how best to explain his sexuality to the Englishman. 'I like both.'

'What's that supposed to mean?'

Pablo shrugged. 'One day I might want to love a man, and then, another day, I might want to love a woman.'
'So you're fifty-fifty then? In England, we call that bisexual.'
'Yes, that is the word... Bisexual.' Pablo turned away and, catching the hot-panted barman's attention, ordered himself a Bacardi and Coke. He looked back at Danny. 'Can I get you a drink?'
'No, it's alright...' Danny felt ill at ease. He hadn't expected to come there and bump into anyone who knew him. 'I'm going after this one.' Danny picked up his beer and started to swig it down at pace.
'There is a good show on in a minute - a comedian. He is very funny. Please... Stay and have a drink with me.'
Danny mulled it over, his thoughts of whether he should stay or go conflicting all the time. The many mirror balls hanging from the ceiling and the strobe lighting that bounced off them every which way just added to Danny's drug-induced brain haze. Then he held up his bottle of San Miguel, 'Alright, Get me another one of these.'
Danny always had time for a good comedian.
...

THE DRAG-QUEEN comedian was indeed very funny, and Danny enjoyed the show. The queen was dressed in a tight, leather mini-skirt and thigh-length leather boots. The bright red hair that hung halfway down the length of his skimpy, glittering halter-top accentuated the large, false eyelashes and heavy make-up. Unusually, Danny thought the comedian was slightly attractive. The drag queen was actually sexier than most women he knew, Danny mused.

Ten minutes after the show was over, Danny needed to urinate and headed for the toilets. He was still a little apprehensive about getting his cock out in front of a load of gay men and decided he'd use a cubicle instead. There were only two cubicles and one was engaged. Danny pushed open the door on what he thought was the free cubicle. He was wide-eyed when confronted with the sight of the drag-queen comedian with his mini-skirt hitched up at waist height and knickers round his ankles. The drag queen was pounding into the rear of another man who, while bent over the toilet, was grabbing the sides of the cistern with both hands. Neither the comedian nor his sexual partner batted an eyelid at Danny's untimely entrance.

The drag queen turned his red-haired head and, seeing Danny's shocked face, winked at him. Then the queen, with no inkling of outward embarrassment, said, 'He's my biggest fan darling.'

Danny hastily retreated, leaving them to it, and took his chances at one of the urinals. He had to wait for a while until his unexpected erection went down, and the urine would flow from his full bladder.

'Ahhh... There she blows.' A groan of sexual satisfaction came from the cubicle as Danny shook

off the last stubborn droplets of urine from his penis.
Danny quickly tucked his manhood back into his pants. He desperately attempted to redirect his thoughts and try to think about something else mundane and completely non-sexual. Danny stood there with his eyes closed, concentrating hard, and, when he was ready, headed back to the bar.

...

'I'LL GET US a drink,' Pablo said as he and Danny entered the small studio apartment that was just a short walk from the gay bar they'd finished the evening in. 'Please make yourself comfortable and sit down.' Pablo gestured toward a low-down, black leather armchair on the far side of the room and headed for the open-plan kitchenette.
Danny went to sit down, but as he was halfway down into the chair, he started to have second thoughts. 'Actually, I think I'd better leave.'
Pablo rushed across the room and gently pushed Danny backwards into the chair. 'No... Please... Please stay. We'll just have a little drink, and then you can go.'
Danny didn't really know what he was doing here. He should have just gone straight back to his own apartment. But the large amount of speed he'd taken meant that he was still buzzing, and even though it was the early hours of the morning, Danny still felt no need for sleep. He looked

around the room suspiciously, with his brain full of racing thoughts of self-doubt and anxiousness. Yes, he liked Pablo – he even found Pablo slightly attractive – but he shouldn't be here.
Towards the end of the evening, Danny and Pablo had got on the dance floor together a couple of times. Danny had taken a lot of prompting, but once out on the floor, he hadn't felt too out of place. Shortly after, Danny had felt Pablo put his hand on his knee and rub his hand up and down his thigh. Danny hadn't objected – he thought he should've done - but he didn't. That had led, shortly after, to Pablo planting a cheeky kiss on Danny's lips. The action had taken Danny by surprise and had made him flinch by turning his face away, but again, for a moment, Danny thought he should've objected - but he didn't.
For some strange reason, Danny's thoughts turned to his father and what he would make of his son's visits to gay bars and ending up alone in a bisexual man's apartment. It was obvious that Pablo wanted Danny tonight, and Danny knew it. *So why was he here?* Danny knew his father would be very disappointed in him. His father would never accept anything other than a heterosexual son. Danny felt a pang of shame - he definitely shouldn't be here - it was a step too far. One quick drink, and then he was going to make his excuses and leave.
'Here you are... Bacardi and Coke. Sorry, it is all I have, so I hope you like Bacardi.' Pablo placed Danny's drink down on a small table by his chair.

'Bacardi's fine.' Pablo hadn't made himself a drink, so it looked like Danny would be drinking alone. 'Where's your drink?' Danny's questioning was slightly agitated as his brain filled with conspiratorial ideas.
'I just need to go to the toilet, then I will make myself a drink, and we will talk.' Pablo disappeared through the bathroom door on the opposite side of the room.
In Pablo's absence, Danny considered leaving there and then. His head was riddled with indecisive, conflicting thoughts. In the end, he opted to take more drugs. He'd do the last of his sulphate, have a drink, and then be off. Danny dug out the packet with his last remaining sulphate in it from his shorts pocket. He licked his finger, dabbed on the open paper packet, and placed his powder-covered index finger on his tongue. The bitter taste almost made him wretch. Then, seeing there was still some residue left in the corners of the packet, he repeated the process until every last speck of powder was gone. Then Danny opened the packet right up and licked the paper just to make sure. Seconds later, he was in need of something to take the bitter taste away and cure his speed-induced, unquenchable thirst, so Danny downed his large Bacardi in one go.
Pablo emerged from the bathroom, and seeing Danny's empty glass, he said, 'You have finished your drink; I'll get you another.'
'Not for me. I'm going to get going now Pablo.'

'No, I insist. Just a little drink and a little talk, and then you can go.'
Danny was reluctant. But, being still full of energy and with the bitter taste that wouldn't leave his mouth, he could easily handle another drink.
'Okay, but that's definitely the last one.'
'Of course... Of course...' Pablo returned to the kitchenette and prepared them both another Bacardi.

...

AS HE SPOKE, Danny could feel his eyes becoming heavy. The conversation had turned to work and Pablo had asked Danny about his job. Danny was only too pleased to enlighten Pablo about his prowess at estate agency. Danny talked non-stop for minutes. He had just started to tell Pablo about his father's offer to start him up with his own agency when he suddenly and inexplicably became overcome with drowsiness. Danny was struggling to keep his eyes open.
Pablo sat sipping at his drink while watching as Danny's eyes closed. Danny's head dropped and he fell into what seemed like a deep sleep.
Pablo had added a little extra something to Danny's drink. After having spent the entire latter part of the evening with this man, Pablo wasn't going to be denied some sexual satisfaction. The "G" had worked well - as it had done many times in the past. Just a tiny amount of the powerful date

rape drug was enough to ensure that Pablo's victims were under his control and at his mercy. Pablo undid his belt, unbuttoned his jeans and went about his business.

...

DANNY WAS GOING in and out of consciousness; it was like he was in a trance. In his subconscious, he wanted to open his eyes, but at this moment in time, it was a physical impossibility. He could feel his head rocking backwards and forwards repeatedly. It was the weirdest sensation. There was a shortness of breath and he felt like he was gagging. *Open you bastards,* Danny's subconscious mind was telling his eyelids.
The sulphate was fighting against the "G". A drug high was battling a drug downer, and Danny, slowly but surely, was starting to come round. Eventually, due to those last few dabs that Danny had taken, the sulphate won the battle of the drugs. The first thing that Danny saw through his flickering eyelids was the sight of Pablo's hairy midriff as he stood over him, and that's what stunned Danny into action. He realised that the cause of the backwards and forward motion of his head was Pablo's pelvic thrusts. The cause of the shortness of breath and the gagging was because Pablo's cock was in his mouth. In an instant, Danny was wide awake and bit down hard. He

heard Pablo's yelp, and then, using all his strength, he threw a right-handed uppercut, jamming his fist into Pablo's balls as hard as he could.
Pablo doubled over in agony - Danny's strike had hit the target bang-on. As Pablo reeled backwards, clutching his groin, Danny pushed himself up from his chair and leapt toward the man who was abusing him. What Danny hadn't realised was that his shorts and underpants were around his ankles, making him stumble forward. Fortunately, Danny fell towards Pablo and they both ended up in a heap on the floor. Pablo was too busy dealing with the agonising pain in his cock and testicles to grapple or provide any resistance. Danny got to his feet, pulled his pants and shorts up and started to kick Pablo viciously in the head.
'YOU FUCKING POOF BASTARD! YOU FUCKING POOF BASTARD! YOU FUCKING POOF BASTARD!' Danny screamed at Pablo with every blow until he could see Pablo wasn't moving anymore and was unconscious. Blood started to trickle from a gash just above Pablo's temple. Danny stood watching as the flow of blood got thicker, became a stream and left a red puddle on the white, tiled floor beside Pablo's head. When Danny was sure that Pablo no longer posed any threat, he fled the scene.

...

A FEW MINUTES into Danny's walk back to the safety of his apartment, a Guardia Civil patrol car slowed down and crawled alongside him for a few metres. The two cap-wearing occupants checked Danny out, suspiciously eyeing him up and down. The sun was just coming up, and there was no one else on the streets. Danny started to panic. *What if Pablo had called the police? What if I've killed him?* To Danny's short-term relief, after a little while, the patrol car picked up speed and disappeared out of sight down a side street.

Eight

Stop the Bus!

Saturday 17th July 1982 – Departure Day...

LYNDSEY'S ALARM WENT off at six o'clock in the morning. She dragged herself out of bed. She was still feeling the after-effects of the booze from the night before. Lyndsey mulled over the events of the previous night's encounter and a wry smile formed on her lips. She shook her head, *silly girl*, she thought. But, at least the pain in her bottom was gone.

Lyndsey took a shower, got dressed and applied her make-up. Sitting at the dressing table, she grabbed some of the hotel's complimentary note paper and wrote a brief letter. Then, she hastily threw the last few remaining clothing items into her suitcase and closed the lid. She was running late, so instead of waiting for the lift, she descended the three flights of stairs at pace, dragging her suitcase, clunking on every step behind her. Lyndsey briefly stopped at reception to hand over her room key and then ran outside to the awaiting taxi.

The driver greeted Lyndsey by tapping his watch and raising his eyebrows to indicate his annoyance at having to wait around for ten minutes due to

Lyndsey's lousy time-keeping. He loaded Lyndsey's case into the trunk and they set off.
As the taxi pulled away, Lyndsey took one last glance back at her hotel. Looking up, she could see the balcony of her third-floor room. Lyndsey turned her gaze back to the road ahead.
One last stop-off at the Beach Rock Bar and then, "Benidorm Lyndsey", would be no more, and Lyndsey Fox, the shy hairdresser from Manchester, would be back in the room.

...

AT SEVEN THIRTY in the morning, Jude took Rascal for one last walk along the beach before too many other revellers were about. Jude threw a ball into the sea for Rascal to fetch and took one last swim in the ocean himself.
Jude and Rascal had become constant companions since their eventful, night-time beach introduction a few nights before. Wherever Jude went, Rascal went too. In the daytime, the dog would lie with Jude around the pool. If Jude headed for the beach, Rascal went too. In the evenings, when Jude hit the bars around town, Rascal would patiently wait outside until Jude was ready to move on, and then Rascal would follow his, by now, master onto the next venue.
Jude fed Rascal three times a day. In the mornings, Rascal would get dry biscuits. Lunch would be a tin of wet dog food, and in the evenings, Jude

would share his own meal with the dog. He had bought Rascal a leash and a collar with a nametag attached to it. Jude had also bought numerous balls and rubber toys for Rascal to chase and entertain himself with.

At night, Rascal (not being allowed into the building itself) slept outside Jude's apartment building. The kindly receptionist had directed Jude to a little cubbyhole behind the dustbins where Rascal could curl up in the nigh-time. Jude purchased a dog bed and some fluffy blankets to keep his newfound pal cosy. For Jude, it was indeed going to be hard to part with the dog, which had become the most loyal and best friend he'd ever had.

The day before, Jude had asked the receptionist if Rascal would be able to stay in his little cubbyhole outside and whether the receptionist could continue to feed the dog if Jude left him some money. The receptionist had told Jude no – if Rascal stayed and his bosses found out, then the receptionist would most likely lose his job. It was okay while Jude was there to look after Rascal, but the dog would have to fend for himself once Jude had gone. The receptionist had done all he could to help and could do no more.

For now, Jude just wanted to enjoy his last hours with Rascal. They continued with their walk along the beach. Jude stopped to take a lie down on the sand and lap up his last taste of Benidorm early-morning sunshine for half an hour with Rascal lying down by his side. Jude tried not to think of what might become of his friend but couldn't stop himself from continually thinking the worst. Jude decided he needed to go shopping to take his mind off things.

...

'THESE ARE FOR you.' Jude lifted a plastic bag from down by his side and plonked it on the table between him and Danny.
Danny pulled the bag slowly towards him while showing very little interest.
'Well, have a look inside then.'
Danny pulled out a shirt and box with a new pair of white Adidas training shoes inside.
'They're from Rascal – he wanted to say sorry.'
Jude laughed.
'Thanks.' There was no emotion in Danny's voice.
'What's up Danny? Something's wrong...You've hardly said a word the last couple of days. Trying to make conversation with you is like getting blood out of a stone.'
Jude and Danny were sitting at a table outside the Beach Rock Bar, getting their last taste of Benidorm beer and some early afternoon sun before catching the coach to the airport.
'What's up? You seem a bit down,' Jude continued – his first question having been ignored.
'I don't want to talk about it.'
'We're mates... You can tell me.'

Danny became agitated, 'I said I don't want to talk about it! Okay?'
'Alright, alright... Calm down... I was just asking.'
'There's nothing you can do about it, so please don't ask any more.'
'Okay... Whatever you say.'
The table fell silent as Danny continued looking down into his beer, twirling his glass round and round between occasional mouthfuls. He couldn't stop thinking about the incident with Pablo. The fact that Pablo hadn't turned up for work at the Beach Rock ever since that fateful night just added to Danny's worries. The kicks that Danny had delivered to Pablo's head were vicious with anger and might have been enough to kill the man. Danny was still raging within about having put himself in such a vulnerable position. He'd been such a fool. Why had he gone to the gay bar? Why had he gone back to Pablo's apartment? Why didn't he leave the apartment when he had the chance? To give himself the slightest comfort, Danny put the blame squarely on the sulphate and the booze because, in truth, he still couldn't admit to himself that there was a possibility he was more gay than straight.
Right now, all Danny wanted to do was get out of Spain. He didn't want to spend time in a Spanish jail for killing a man who had sexually assaulted him.
'Looking forward to going home then?' Micky, the short, stocky, fortyish, pony-tailed bar manager at the Beach Rock, asked in a strong Scottish accent

as he went about collecting up the empty glasses at a table close by. Micky had got to know Jude and Danny quite well during their frequent visits to his bar.
'No, not really. And, I'm especially not looking forward to leaving him.' Jude patted Rascal, the dog, on his head as he lay down obediently beside Jude's feet.
'Yeah, that's a tough one...' Micky deposited the empty glasses on the bar and walked over to Jude and Danny's table. Micky got down on his knees and started stroking Rascal's white-striped head and jet-black back. 'I'd consider taking him on myself, but my missus is allergic to dogs, so it's out of the question.' Micky got back to his feet, 'Anyway, I've got something for you, Jude...' Micky went behind the bar and, after rummaging around under the counter, returned with an envelope with Jude's name written on it. 'I found this pushed under the shutter this morning... It's for you. Micky handed over the envelope and then continued, 'Oh, and that fucking Pablo...'
'What about Pablo?' Danny, startled by the mention of his abuser's name, butted in immediately. Danny hung on with dread before hearing the rest of what Micky had to say.
'He phoned up Friday morning and said he can't come to work for a week.'
Danny's pent-up anxiety dissipated at the news Pablo was still alive. Danny was a free man and could fly back to England without fear.

'Said he'd fallen over and bashed his head badly... Or something like that... I wasn't really listening to be honest. The thing is, I was going to sack him anyway. I found out he was dipping his hands in the till. So, he's history now anyway, and there's a job going if anyone wants it.' Micky pointed at Jude, 'You'd do well at it I reckon. Good-looking boy like you. The pay isn't great, but the job does have its benefits; you'll get hold of loads of birds, and there's the extra bonus of free drinks on your day off.'

Before Jude could respond, the most beautiful apparition of a female with lightly tanned skin, long black hair and perfectly formed features came into view. She wore a thin, white throw with a contrasting black bikini underneath. Jude thought she was the most beautiful thing he had ever seen. The apparition sneaked behind Micky and, wrapping her arms around him, planted a kiss on his cheek.

'Hi Dad,' the apparition said. The apparition's voice was as soft as her perfect skin.

'Hi gorgeous. Go and grab a seat and I'll be over for a chat in a second.'

The apparition headed inside the bar.

'That's your daughter?'

'Yeah.'

'What's her name?'

'Isabella. But don't even think about it, mate.'

'What, because I'm black?'

Micky gave Jude a playful slap around the top of his head. 'Fuck off... It's nothing like that. It's not

me mate, it's her mother... Spanish and very protective. One lash of her tongue can kill a man at ten paces.' Micky walked away laughing.
Jude couldn't take his eyes off the beautiful apparition. Feeling he should stop staring and embarrassed by his infatuation, to distract himself, he decided to open the envelope that Micky had given him and pulled out the hand-written letter inside:

Dear Jude,
I'll be on my plane home by the time you get this letter and I hope you're not upset with me for not saying goodbye.
I just wanted you to know that I think you're lovely bloke and I really enjoyed our time together.
After the threesome thing, I suppose you think I'm a bit of a slag, but I can assure you that isn't the case. I'm not looking for sympathy, but my life hasn't been easy the last few years, and I came away on my own to get away and escape reality for a while. The person you met on holiday isn't the real me.
On holiday, I wanted to do things I'd never done before and be someone I hadn't been before. I wanted to do those things and be that person without being judged by others. I hope you can understand
Have a nice life.
Lots of love,
Lyndsey xx.

...

‘GOODBYE MY BEST buddy.’ Jude knelt down, his arms wrapped around Rascal’s muscular neck with their cheeks rubbing against each other.
‘You’re going to have to find someone else to look after you.’ Jude was trying hard not to get tearful, but this was one of the hardest moments of his life.
Rascal raised his paws from the ground and planted them squarely on Jude’s shoulders. Then Jude’s tears came.
‘Try to find someone like me... Someone who’ll be your best friend.’ Jude pulled away and looked into the dog’s brown eyes. ‘Stay safe buddy.’ Rascal licked him on the face.
The female tour rep was watching from the step of the open coach front doors. ‘I’m sorry, but we really *do* have to leave now’.
Jude got to his feet and started to slowly back away from Rascal. ‘Look after yourself boy. Thanks for being my friend.’
Rascal cocked his head to one side, his ear’s pricked up and there was a lost, sad look in his big eyes.
Jude forced his eyes away from Rascal’s longing gaze and stepped onto the coach. Jude couldn’t resist glancing back at his best friend one last time before the doors closed behind him.
Jude walked quickly down the aisle and took his seat next to Danny, and the coach started to pull away.

If there was one positive Jude could take from the current situation, it was that Danny's mood had suddenly brightened, and he was more or less back to his old self. Jude didn't have a clue why. It was like the world's weight had been lifted from Danny's shoulders. The only thing Jude could come up with for a reason as to Danny's rapid change in attitude was that, perhaps, Danny really didn't like the dog. Perhaps Danny was glad to see the back of Rascal.
As the coach rolled forward, Jude was determined not to look back. He only managed to be true to himself for a few seconds until he couldn't help himself and jumped out of his seat. Jude leaned over Danny and peered out the window. Jude saw Rascal was following on behind. First at walking pace, and then, as the coach picked up speed, Rascal started to run. Shortly, the dog was right under the window where he could see his master's face.
Jude noticed with concern Rascal was getting too close to the coach's wheels and tried to shout instructions from the coach's high-up, quarter-light window. 'RASCAL YOU'RE TOO CLOSE... GET AWAY BOY!'
Feeling Jude's panic, some of the other coach passengers were by now starting to get out of their seats and take notice of the scene unravelling below.
The angle of view, as Rascal got closer to the side of the vehicle, became too acute and the dog disappeared from sight. A second later, the

thudding noise coming from under the floor as something hit the underside of the coach made Jude feel sick. The noise rapidly travelled down the coach towards the rear. Jude felt the coach's rear wheel rise from the ground as it went over something solid in the road. There was a crunching and cracking sound that was audible even from the inside of the coach.
'JESUS CHRIST!' Jude was beside himself, 'STOP THE BUS!' He bolted down the aisle to the front of the coach. 'STOP THE BUS!'

...

THE COACH'S DOORS were barely open before Jude, in his sheer panic, squeezed himself through them. He sprinted to the back of the vehicle. There was no sign of Rascal. Jude took a deep breath before apprehensively lowering himself to the ground and taking a look under the wheels. He was relieved at seeing the empty space between the coach's underside and the road, but there was still no sign of his canine friend.
Jude got back to his feet and looked down the road. He saw a round, half-crushed plastic bin with all its contents of food cartons and drink bottles strewn over the carriageway. Then, as his brain was racing away with him, Jude stumbled forward from the force of the shove in the middle of his back that had come out of nowhere. He turned around.

‘RASCAL!’ Jude sank to his knees. His relief was overwhelming. Jude grabbed Rascal’s head and gave the dog a kiss.
Rascal, running at pace and with his vision focussed on Jude at the window, had not spotted the pavement bin that lay in his path. The dog had hit the bin at full pace. It was the bin that Rascal had pushed into the coach’s path and been crushed under its wheels. Rascal was unharmed.
For the time being, pending Jude’s decision, Rascal and his master were joyously reunited.

...

‘THIS IS DUMB... Really dumb.’ Danny watched as Jude pulled his suitcase from the coach’s luggage compartment
‘No, it’s not dumb Danny. It’s going to be the best thing I’ve ever done - I know it is.’
‘You need to come home.’
Jude plonked the suitcase down on the pavement and looked into Danny’s eyes intently. ‘Home? What’s fucking home? A home that’s a tiny room in someone else’s house... A home with no job... A home with a mother who’s so pissed all the time she couldn’t give a shit whether I’m alive or dead... A home where I’ve got fucking nothing and fucking no one.’
‘You’ve got me and Brian,’ Danny smiled.

‘Yeah, sorry I didn’t mean any offence. Look out for Brian for me. Tell him I’m sorry, and I’ll see him soon.’

‘Will do.’

‘I can’t leave Rascal. I can’t just leave him to fend for himself. He needs me, and, to be honest, I need him. He’s been the only stable thing I’ve had in my life for a long, long time.’

‘What are you going to do?’

‘I’m going to take Micky up on that offer of the bar job.’ Jude raised his arms toward the bright, blue Benidorm sky. ‘Look Danny... This is fucking paradise to me... This is home.’ Jude stepped forward and got Danny in a bear hug. ‘See you later mate. Look after yourself.’

‘And you mate.’ Danny walked away and boarded the coach. Taking his seat, Danny gave Jude a final goodbye wave as the coach pulled away.

Jude grabbed the handle of his suitcase, turned around and headed for the Beach Rock, suitcase on one side and Rascal on the other. Jude’s thoughts turned to accommodation. He needed somewhere to stay. Micky would help him. Micky would know somewhere - somewhere where they allowed dogs.

Epilogue

Lyndsey

Three months after Lyndsey's return from Benidorm, Sebastian turned up on her doorstep unannounced. It turned out that he really did love Lyndsey and begged her to try again. Sebastian had changed his ways, cleaned up his act and (with his parents' agreement) had changed his course at university. He was now doing a degree in computer science.

Lyndsey and Sebastian were married in 1987. Unfortunately, Lyndsey's dad (Terry) couldn't make it to the wedding as he was doing another stretch in jail. His luck had run out, and he was banged up for armed robbery.

Sebastian got his timing right. And, with the explosion of personal computers in the late eighties and early nineties, he set up his own computer consultancy company and made a fortune.

Lyndsey and Sebastian went on to have two children and now live in California, USA. Lyndsey's time in Benidorm was never mentioned.

Jude

Jude took up Micky's job offer at the Beach Rock Bar. Soon after, Jude and Micky's daughter (the apparition) started dating. They remain together until the present day and have three children.
In 1986, Jude's mother, due to her alcoholism, died of liver failure. Jude decided not to return to the UK for her funeral.

Jude and Rascal remained best friends and constant companions. Rascal became a feature in the Beach Rock Bar and enjoyed the attention of thousands of customers. Rascal led a happy and active life until his death from lung cancer in 1988. Jude was devastated.

Rascal's ashes are scattered along the stretch of beach outside the Beach Rock Bar.
In 1991, Jude and Micky moved on from The Beach Rock and (using Jude's knowledge of the market) started their own company supplying sanitary products. Their company now delivers *bog rolls* and other sanitary supplies to hotels, restaurants and bars all over the Costa Blanca.

Danny

After his experiences in Benidorm, Danny decided to abstain from all forms of sexual activity. And, rather than admit that he was attracted to other men, Danny classed himself as asexual.

Danny's dad was true to his word and gave Danny the money to start his own estate agency. During the mid to late-eighties housing price boom, Danny's company went from strength to strength. In 1989, he diversified away from estate agency into property and, borrowing large amounts of money from banks, invested heavily in buying properties to renovate and resell.

Unfortunately, come the nineties, the market crashed and Danny was left high and dry. The banks called in their debts, repossessed his properties and Danny lost everything.

With what cash he had left, Danny turned further to drugs. He became addicted to crack cocaine and then to heroin. He died of an overdose in 1995.

Brian

When they got back from Brighton, Brian and Sharon went house hunting. By putting their Funds together, they managed to put down a deposit on a two-bedroom house.

Brian and Sharon got married in the summer of 1983, and having decided to take their honeymoon there, Brian finally made it to Benidorm. Brian and Sharon now return to Benidorm every year to visit Jude and his family.

Brian rose quickly from supermarket shelf-stacker to managing his own store within a few years of his chance meeting with Sharon.

Brian's Uncle Kevin had a mild stroke in 1997, which meant he had difficulty making it up the stairs up to his second-floor flat. Brian decided that it was only fair to repay the commitment to look after *him* that Kevin had made to his father all those years ago and invited his uncle to stay at his house. Kevin sold his apartment and moved in with Brian and Sharon. They looked after Kevin until his death in 2003.

Despite lots of practice and trying, Brian and Sharon weren't able to have any children.

THE END

Printed in Great Britain
by Amazon

35827812R00079